MURDERED
BY
MOONLIGHT

MURDERED
BY
MOONLIGHT

Roger Keevil

a Ramston murder mystery

also by Roger Keevil

THE INSPECTOR CONSTABLE MURDER MYSTERIES

Murderer's Fête
Murder Unearthed
Death Sails In The Sunset
Murder Comes To Call
Murder Most Frequent
The Odds On Murder
No Bar To Murder
The Murder Cabinet
The Game Of Murder

THE COPPER & CO MURDER MYSTERIES

Honeymooner's Murder
Murder At Witch's Holt
Buccaneer's Murder

MURDERED BY MOONLIGHT

by

Roger Keevil

Cover design by Christopher Brooke

'Gentles, perchance you wonder at this show.
Then wonder on, till truth makes all things plain.'

Chapter 1
Friday

"Are you sure you've loaded everything?" asked Tania Faye for what seemed like the umpteenth time.

"Absolutely positive," replied Ron firmly, closing the car's tailgate with a fairly restrained slam. "And anything we haven't got, we can buy when we're down there. They do have shops in Cornwall, you know. And it's not as if it's for the rest of our lives. It's only ten days."

"And you've got the paperwork for the cottage?"

Ron reached in through the driver's door, picked up a folder, and brandished it in his wife's direction. "Everything's in here. Emails, receipts, directions, and the postcode for the satnav in case we get hopelessly confused and end up in some farmer's field."

Tania stepped closer to her husband and put her arms around him. "I don't know what I'd do without you."

"Rubbish!" retorted Ron robustly. "You know perfectly well you're a far better organiser than I am. You've done all the packing. I just put the stuff in the car. Although," he remarked, "I can't quite see why we seem to be taking enough food to feed an army. Is there some sort of famine on the other side of the Tamar? Surely we can always nip off to the local pub for a pint and a pasty."

"It's just to be on the safe side," said Tania. "We're bound to be keeping odd hours over the next few days, so I thought we ought to have a few ready meals we can just bung in the microwave. And a lot of the other stuff is for the party after the show on the first night. I've already told everyone that it's back to ours after the performance. I mean, it's expected. We are both playing the leads."

"Funny," chuckled Ron. "All these years with the

Society, and it's the first time we've played husband and wife."

"And not just any old husband and wife," replied Tania. "King and Queen of Fairyland, I would remind you. And doubled up with Theseus and Hippolyta too. No riff-raff. I think that deserves some sort of special celebration."

"And double the lines to learn," groaned Ron in mock complaint. "I'm still having trouble with that *'I know a bank'* speech. I keep swapping the plants about."

"You'll be fine," his wife reassured him. "Anyway, if that's your only problem, I shouldn't worry. We don't open until next Wednesday. That's a whole five days to get them under your belt."

Ron looked at his watch. "And if we don't make a start, it'll be down to four days. Cornwall's not just a five minute drive, you know."

Tania gave him a peck on the cheek. "We'd best get going then. I'll lock up while you start the car, and we'll hit the road." And only moments later she was settling in alongside him, as Ron backed out of the drive and headed for the motorway.

*

When Grace and Mickey Waite had started the Ramston Players in the immediate aftermath of the Second World War, they had no inkling that their brainchild would develop a life of its own. Initially planned as an outlet for Grace's no-longer-wanted talents as a performer with ENSA, now that the arrival of peace meant that the armed forces had less need of entertainment to take their minds off the rigours of conflict, the amateur dramatic society was also inspired by tales of the jolly concerts performed to lift spirits in the prisoner-of-war camps, as told by Mickey's recently-released former RAF colleagues. Friends were recruited by the newly-weds, rehearsals were held in a disused

Nissen hut in the grounds of the local church, and their first production, a light Noël Coward comedy, was greeted with great acclaim on opening night in the small town's Memorial Hall. Now, over three-quarters of a century later, the group had grown beyond all recognition. Renamed the Ramston Operatic And Dramatic Society after a first venture into musical theatre in the early 1950s, with a production of Gilbert and Sullivan's 'The Mikado' in which Grace and Mickey stole the audience's hearts as Yum-Yum and Nanki-Poo, the society now had over a hundred members and was able to tackle several shows a year. From the darkest thrillers to the most whimsical of musical comedies, all were performed in the group's own theatre, a superannuated small local cinema acquired in the 1970s through a substantial bequest from a former member, refurbished through a massive effort by the members of R.O.A.D.S., renamed the Waite Theatre in tribute to the late founding couple, and run as a charity by the Society's committee.

The group was held in high esteem for the quality of its productions, and its renown had spread – so much so, that this year, a highly-coveted invitation had been received to perform at the annual summer festival by the trustees of the celebrated Mandyke Open-Air Theatre in Cornwall. There was lengthy discussion as to the choice of show, before a suggestion by Grace and Mickey's granddaughter had clinched the decision.

"It's scheduled for the end of June," Tania had pointed out. "In fact, isn't the opening night going to be on the twenty-first? So isn't it obvious? It's got to be 'A Midsummer Night's Dream'." And so auditions were held under the severe gaze of director Leah Sutherland, and a cast was announced.

"I hope nobody thinks I suggested the play because I was trying to pull rank and get a part," Tania confided in a whisper to Ron at the first read-through.

"Don't be daft," murmured Ron in response. "You got the part fair and square. Anyone can see that. I doubt if half the younger members even have a clue that Grace Waite was your grandmother. And even if they did, didn't Leah tell you that she can see a whole lot of Grace in you? And she knew her for years. Anyway, I can't see anyone trying to put one over on that particular dragon. She scares me to death."

"Shhh!" giggled Tania. "She'll hear you. And anyway, you should be grateful. She did cast us together."

"I know. I am grateful really. And to tell the truth, I am actually very fond of the old trout. But you must admit, she is pretty intimidating."

"Good. It keeps some of the naughtier kids under control." Tania smiled. "Including you. Now be quiet. We're starting."

*

"I hope there aren't any hold-ups on the way," remarked Ron as he turned left at the end of their Close. "It's a long enough drive as it is."

"Hold on a second, and I'll check the traffic app," replied Tania, burrowing in her bag for her phone. "It's not going to start things off on the right foot if we have to spend hours sitting in traffic jams." After a few moments she sighed with relief. "You'll be pleased to hear, not a sausage. No major roadworks en route, and no reports of any accidents. In fact, sunshine and smiles all the way."

"Then let's hope it stays like that."

The journey west unfolded. Under a virtually cloudless sky, suburbs faded into countryside, motorway gave way eventually to dual carriageway and then almost clear main roads, which carved a steady undeviating path over rolling chalk downs and between fields studded with grazing sheep or filled with ripening crops in varying shades of green and gold.

"Do you think we ought to take a break for a bit?" suggested Tania after a couple of hours of uneventful progress. "We could stop for elevenses somewhere, and then I could take over the driving for a while. After all, you can't be expected to drive the whole way in one go."

"You'll get no arguments from me," agreed Ron. "In fact ... hang on a minute. I've got an idea."

"What?"

Ron gave a secret smile. "You'll see." After just over a mile, he turned off to the left, on to a minor country road which twisted its way southwards between high hedge-crowned banks.

"The satnav doesn't like it," commented Tania, as the navigation device mounted on the dashboard repeated an increasingly insistent instruction to *'Turn around now'*.

"Pay no attention," grinned Ron. "She'll get fed up soon enough. In fact ... there you go." He nodded towards the screen. "She's *'Recalculating'*. She ought to know by now, I don't respond well to nagging." And in response to a meaningful throat-clearing from alongside him, "Not that you ever nag me, dearest."

"Hmmm," was Tania's response. "Anyway, you still haven't told me. Where are we going?"

"What, don't you recognise where we are? You remember, we came down and stayed around here for a weekend a few years ago. That funny old-fashioned hotel in the town on the coast, where all the guests were about a hundred and fifty. And I recall one place we visited where we had a very nice cream tea after we'd met some of the extremely friendly residents."

After a few moments, Tania's puzzled frown disappeared, and she gave a delighted laugh. "Of course! The donkey sanctuary! Oh, that was lovely."

"And I seem to recall that they had some very delicious-looking gateaux in their cafe. Not to mention the provision of some very useful facilities. Let's hope things haven't changed." A few minutes later, a brown roadside sign gave notice that they were approaching their destination, and Ron steered the car into a narrow lane and drew up in the gravelled car park at the end, among a scatter of other cars. "Now, tea and cake first, I think," he said, uncoiling himself from behind the steering wheel and stretching. "And then maybe we can renew a couple of old acquaintances before we get on our way once more."

After doing justice to a generous pot of good strong English Breakfast tea, accompanied by gigantic slices of a lemon drizzle cake which more than lived up to expectations, the couple met up as they emerged simultaneously from the conveniences next to the cafe.

"I definitely needed that," said Ron. "In all respects. In fact, don't the royal family have a saying about never missing an opportunity to sit down, or a chance to go to the loo?"

"I believe," said Tania in exaggeratedly prim tones, as the two made their way down the path towards the stables and barns of the old original farmstead, "that in royal circles, it is discreetly listed on the schedule as an 'Opportunity To Powder'."

"I never knew you were so chummy with the Queen," grinned Ron. "But I suppose it will all come in handy for your part in the play."

Passing through the gate which led to the stable yard, the couple were met by the sight of a small group of donkeys clustered around a small girl, who was squealing with delight as they nuzzled each other aside to gather their own portion from a bucket of donkey nuts which she held under the watchful supervision of a member of staff. Other animals looked out over their stable doors, placidly nodding, seemingly content that their turn would come.

"Oh, look at this one, Ron," exclaimed Tania, as she approached one of the protruding heads, that of a small white donkey whose neck collar declared her to be 'Rosey'. "Isn't she gorgeous?" She scratched the ears of the beast, which responded by leaning in towards her, its eyes half-closed in apparent ecstasy.

"Hold on," said Ron, fumbling in Tania's bag for her phone. "Now, don't move a muscle." Click. "There. Take a look at that." He held out the phone for Tania to inspect the resultant photo. "You can use that as inspiration for your love scene with Bottom."

Tania laughed. "Actually, now you come to mention it, this donkey does look a bit like Andrew. Maybe I should run through my lines with Rosey now."

"Fun thought, but time's getting on," pointed out Ron. "We haven't got all day. There's a long way to go. So back to the car, I think, and you can do the next stint of driving if you like. And then I'll take over again when we hit Cornwall."

"Sounds like a plan," said Tania, and with one farewell scratch of Rosey's ears, she led the way through the gate and back towards the car.

*

There was a subtle but distinct change to the atmosphere of the landscape as the couple's route took them further into England's most south-westerly county. Tree-shaded valleys alternated with glimpses of high heather-covered moors, and hedgerows became less frequent as the number of low field-encircling stone walls increased. Here and there, the chimney of a long-abandoned tin mine reared its crumbling crown on the horizon. From time to time, a distant sparkle seen out of the corner of the eye indicated that the coast was growing ever closer. And eventually, as the time to their destination reduced on the satnav display to single figures, the device gave an instruction to turn into a narrow winding lane flanked by steep banks.

"I just hope we don't come face to face with a tractor," remarked Ron, as the car descended. And suddenly, after the lane seemed to shake itself and turn a sudden corner, the road broadened out to a more comfortable width, and a sign on the verge announced 'Welcome to Polkernow', as the outskirts of the village came into view. Moments later came the disembodied announcement - *'You have arrived at your destination'*. "And here we are – Fore Street. And that, I think ..." He pointed as he drew to a halt. "... is our cottage."

"Ron, isn't it lovely?" breathed Tania.

"That," agreed her husband, "is even better than the picture on the net."

The couple climbed out of the car and stood looking at the cottage before them. Granite-built, with a higgledy-piggledy slate roof with tiny dormer windows peeping out from it, the cottage was long and low, seeming to settle back into the hillside which rose behind it. A slightly rickety white-painted gate led through the low stone wall enclosing a small front garden filled with old-fashioned flowers, while to one side of the building, a sturdier-looking five-bar gate gave access to a gravelled parking spot.

"And it's even got roses round the door," marvelled Tania. "I can't wait to get inside."

"Just one second," said Ron, reaching back into the car and producing the file of paperwork. "According to this, the key is ..." He browsed the instructions and chuckled. "Under the flowerpot on the front doorstep. They're obviously not too hot on security round here," he added with a laugh. "Just imagine if we did that at home. You'd come in one day and find the house had been stripped bare."

"I'm taking it as a good sign," retorted Tania. "Obviously it means that the people round here are all nice and trustworthy."

The interior of the cottage proved to be no disappointment. A snug beamed living room, cosy with plump chintzy sofas, watercolour prints of local scenery, and a wood-burning stove in an enormous fireplace adorned with a gleaming brass kettle, gave in one direction on to a tiny study lined with bookshelves, and in the other to a kitchen which combined modern stainless steel appliances with traditional oak cabinets and an old-style butler's china sink. Beyond that lay a small utility room and a cloakroom, with a back door leading out to the parking space. And on the kitchen table stood a wicker basket containing a bottle of cider, a paper bag of scones, a pot of jam and a tub of clotted cream, a pack of Original biscuits, a box of teabags, and a note saying *Welcome to Hollyhock Cottage. There's milk in the fridge. I hope you enjoy your stay. Mary Pengelly.*

"See what I mean?" said Tania. "And look, there's a folder here ..." She opened it and swiftly browsed the contents. "... with all sorts of local information. Including a map of the village showing where the theatre is. Shall we go and have a look?" she enquired excitedly.

"First things first," replied Ron. "I'll put the car in, and I'll unload our stuff and put the food in the fridge while you make a cup of tea. Didn't you do some sandwiches?"

"I thought we might need something to eat on the way. I wasn't sure how long it would take us to get here."

Ron looked at his watch. "I did wonder if we might find the local pub and try for some lunch there, but it's probably a bit late. So why don't we have a snack now, and then we'll have a scout around afterwards. We can find the theatre *and* suss out the pub."

"Sounds good to me," said Tania. She opened one of the kitchen cabinets. "Now ... mugs."

*

"I'll tell you one thought that occurs to me," said Ron, as the couple strolled hand-in-hand down the picturesque village street. "That cottage is beautiful, and perfect for the pair of us, but I can't see how we're going to fit in the entire cast of the play for a first-night party."

"You could be right," agreed Tania. "We'll think of something. In the meantime, look. Here's the sign. The theatre's down this way."

At the end of a side lane stood an imposing house. Stark white, it was an unexpected and impressive statement of the Art Deco style, with sweeping curved outlines contrasting with angular details in window frames and balustrades. As the couple approached, a young man in his thirties emerged from the front door, locking it behind him and shutting out the faint sound of high-pitched yapping from within, before turning to the newcomers with a look of enquiry on his face.

"Can I help you?"

"We're looking for the theatre," explained Ron. "We've just arrived. We're from Ramston. We're in next week's play."

"Great," smiled the other, extending a hand. "I'm Luke ... Luke Crowan. I'm the Front-of-House Manager for the theatre. Would you like to come round to take a look at it?"

"If it's no trouble," said Tania. "We wouldn't want to get in anyone's way."

"Oh, that's no problem," said Luke. "There's nobody down at the theatre at the moment. They won't be here for tonight's performance until later. But I can take you round to have a look from the back, if you like. You can't go down on to the stage, I'm afraid, because the other group's stuff is all there, but you can get an idea of things." He cast a momentary, and for some reason a seemingly slightly wary look towards the upper windows of the house, before leading the way around the side of the building and through a gate, emerging on to a terrace at the rear. "Well, there you are."

Tania and Ron stood, lost for words. The view before them was astonishing. Below their feet, tumbling away from the very edge of the terrace, lay the theatre, the banks of seating nestling in a natural curving hollow in the cliff, enhanced here and there by balconies and niches carved out of the rock or built up with the subtle use of concrete. At the foot of the auditorium lay the stage area, an irregular platform consisting of several levels dotted with monoliths and square arches, screened to provide exits and entrances. And at the back of the stage, nothing. The backdrop was the horizon itself. The cliff fell precipitously to the sparkling waters of Polkernow Bay far below, with ... was that really a pod of dolphins visible amongst the waves? Away to the right, the dramatic granite finger of Lizard Point thrust itself out into the English Channel, a magnet for groups of tourists who, throughout the holiday season, queued to scramble their way to its uttermost tip to stake their claim to be the most southerly person on the British mainland. And in the distance to the east, a smudge on the skyline was testimony to the presence of Bolt Head at Devon's southern extremity.

"You realise," murmured Tania after several long moments, "that with this to contend with, nobody's going to be watching us act."

Ron put his arm round his wife's waist and drew her to him. "I wouldn't be so sure. With your dazzling talent, the audience won't be able to keep their eyes off you."

Chapter 2
Friday

"And that," announced Ron with satisfaction, "is that." He pushed the wardrobe door closed, and it swung to with a gentle squeak. "And I suppose we'll get used to all these squeaks and creaks eventually."

Tania looked up from putting the final items away in the chest of drawers alongside the bed. "I think it all adds to the charm of the place."

"Let's see how charming I think it is after I've cracked my head a few more times on that beam over the bathroom door," remarked Ron.

"The people who built this cottage probably weren't expecting it to be occupied by somebody who's six feet tall," pointed out Tania.

"Maybe I could borrow Theseus' war helmet to wear around the house. That'd cut down the chances of getting concussion and forgetting all my lines. Do you reckon Leah would be up for that?"

"Not a chance," laughed Tania. "From what she was saying, she's not letting the costumes out of her sight until dress rehearsal. And I don't blame her, after all the work the wardrobe team did in making them."

"I still don't see why one of the wardrobe people couldn't come down to look after them. After all, it isn't as if Leah hasn't got enough to do."

"Apparently nobody could get away. Something to do with holidays already booked."

"I suppose if Leah is happy to do it, who's going to stand in her way? Certainly not me!"

"True." Tania surveyed the bedroom. "I think this is all very snug and romantic. I'm looking forward to this week. So, what next?"

"Here's a thought. Why don't I go and put the kettle on, and we'll see off those scones, just to keep our strength up until we can go out for something to eat this evening. And you can take a look at the WhosUp group to see if anybody else has made it down here yet." Ron made his way out on to the tiny landing and down the creaky winding stairs, which emerged into a corner of the living room.

As the couple sat sipping tea at the scrubbed pine table in the kitchen, a few crumbs on the plate before them the only evidence of the existence of the scones in question, Tania scrolled through her phone. "Well, David and Elizabeth Kent and the kids have made it."

"Didn't David say they've organised a caravan or some such?"

"Yes. There's a holiday park at the other end of the village, apparently, so they've booked a big van there."

"They're going to need it with four boys to cope with."

"I think Elizabeth's hoping that the kids will tire themselves out in the pool or the play area, so they won't have enough energy to cause their usual mayhem during the show."

"I blame Shakespeare," smiled Ron. "If he hadn't given the Fairy Queen four attendants, you wouldn't have the job of trying to keep them under control. Maybe you can exercise some of your magical powers."

"Or else threats of dire consequences if they play up," muttered Tania darkly.

"Anyone else?"

"Peter and Martha Talbot put up a posting a couple of hours ago saying they were on their way. They're staying in another cottage somewhere in the village, but I don't know where."

"How about Susannah?" wondered Ron.

"Oh, she's staying with them," replied Tania. "You don't think they'd let their seventeen-year-old daughter go off under her own steam, do you?"

"Not if I know anything about teenagers," said Ron wryly. "Speaking of which, what about Thomas and James?"

"They're sharing a tent at the holiday park. I think the idea was to keep them under the watchful eye of David and Elizabeth, according to Thomas's mother."

"Good luck with that," laughed Ron. "They'll have enough to do, trying to control their own brood. Is that it?"

"Almost. Leah's coming down tonight. She's renting a flat over the village teashop, she told me. And Andrew is putting up at the pub. He's on his way, so he says here. And Esther and Sarah, and Paul and Timothy, are coming down in the morning. They're staying at the pub as well."

"Sharing rooms?" Ron raised an eyebrow. "Very appropriate for the lovers."

"I believe," said Tania, failing to conceal a smile, "that the girls are sharing one room, and the boys are sharing another. At least, that's the official version. I don't like to ask questions."

"Best not to," nodded Ron. "So, that's everyone accounted for. Any idea when we all get together?"

Tania checked the screen. "Leah says there'll be a meeting in the morning. She's going to message us all with details as soon as she knows."

"In which case," said Ron, gathering up the tea things and moving over to the sink, "the rest of the evening's our own. I'll wash these bits and pieces up, and we can carry on exploring."

*

Polkernow turned out to be everything that a picturesque Cornish village ought to be. Off the main street, side roads with faded wooden signs such as that pointing to 'Penwalloe's Farm' tended to peter out into rutted tracks ending in open five-bar gates with old abandoned wooden carts gently mouldering in the long grass alongside them. An ancient church dedicated to the local saint huddled in a sheltered hollow, its precincts dotted with moss-covered gravestones and tombs beneath the canopy of an enormous and venerable yew tree. Alongside St. Petroc's church, a twisting lane signposted 'Harbour' descended towards the sea, where a tiny breakwater sheltering a handful of fishing boats could be glimpsed. The main street itself was lined with stone cottages, mostly set back a little from the road behind pretty flower-filled gardens, while several whose fronts gave directly on to the street had been turned into business premises. A shop whose Georgian-paned window was empty, save for a large white marble slab occupied by the figurine of a jolly-looking pig in a straw hat and a stripey apron, proudly proclaimed itself to be 'Tresillian's Family Butchers'. 'The Piskey's Cavern' displayed a mixture of souvenirs ranging from the tasteful and expensive to the depressingly twee. 'Hawke's Hardware' showed a no-nonsense range of tools, saucepans and gardening requisites behind its workmanlike plate glass, while the shop sign also advertised the provision of livestock feed, domestic fuel, key-cutting and shoe repairs. And next door, a diamond-paned bow window dressed with frilled lace and chintz curtains featured a silver tray bearing an elegant setting of teacup and saucer, milk jug, sugar bowl and teapot, all in the most ornate flowery Victorian style, with a three-tier cake-stand sporting a slightly dusty-looking selection of finger sandwiches, scones, and cakes.

"Those look exactly like the scones we had for tea," observed Ron.

"They obviously came from here," said Tania. "Except that ours were lovely and fresh. I'm hoping that those are just props for window-dressing. Because the place looks charming." She looked up at the sign above the shop front, and perused the menu displayed alongside the entrance. "'A Cake and a Cuppa', they're called. And it looks from this as if they live up to their name. There's more cakes listed here than you can shake a fork at. Including vegan ones. And they do cream teas. I'm definitely up for one of those."

"Well, we've got a week to take advantage," said Ron. "But in the meantime, I've got something more substantial in mind. My insides are starting to rumble. And it looks to me as if we've got just the place across the road. And that," he added, "is a very inviting-looking pub."

The Pilchard's Arms was the most notable building on the main street of Polkernow. Three storeys of impressive dressed stonework rose to a crenellated crown, with elegantly symmetrical sash windows with a scatter of bottle-glass panes giving forth a warm and welcoming glow. Through an arch to one side of the building, a cobbled yard could be seen. Three semicircular steps at the front led up to a pillared portico, while above the entrance hung a sign with a whimsical representation of a pilchard clad in fisherman's oilskins and sou'wester, a foaming tankard of ale clutched in one of its brawny arms. And a signboard alongside the front door announced the availability of morning coffees, lunches, and evening meals.

"I think we've found somewhere you can satisfy your longing for a pie and a pasty," smiled Tania.

"I'm hoping we can do better than that," said Ron. "After you." He ushered his wife up the steps and into the entrance hall, to find a small desk marked 'Reception' and an elaborately-carved staircase in dark oak leading to the upper floors. A door to the left was marked 'Lounge Bar', and Ron held it back for Tania to enter.

"Evening, my loves!" came the immediate cheery greeting from behind the bar. A motherly-looking woman

22

in her fifties, comfortably plump and with dark hair above startlingly blue eyes and rosy cheeks, gave the newcomers a swift up-and-down look before asking, "Now, what can I get you?"

"Is it possible to get something to eat?" enquired Tania.

"Course it is, my dear," came the robust reply. "Let me get you some drinks first, and then you can think about food."

After ordering a gin-and-tonic for Tania and a pint for Ron - "You try the Tintagel Tun, my love – you won't be disappointed" was the barmaid's suggestion – Tania enquired if it was possible to see a menu.

"Tell you what, my dear. You go and settle yourselves down in one of those booths, and I'll bring your drinks and the menu over to you." And moments later, as the barmaid placed the drinks on the table, she enquired brightly, "Staying around here, are you?"

"Yes, actually," said Ron. "We've come down to do a play at the theatre."

"I knew it!" exclaimed the barmaid. "I can always tell the theatricals. So much nicer than the rest of the emmets who come cluttering our lanes up in the summer."

"Emmets?" enquired Tania.

"It's what we call the tourists, my love. The ones who come in, poke around the place, and then leave without spending any money."

"I thought tourists were called 'grockles'," queried Ron.

"No, love. That's what they say over in England." A smile. "Or Devon, as you'd call it. But round here it's 'emmets'. It's Cornish for ants. So, where are you staying?"

"In a place at the top of the village," said Tania. "It's called Hollyhock Cottage."

"Oh, that's one of mine!" was the delighted reply. "You must be Mr and Mrs Faye."

"We are," smiled Ron.

"I'm Mary. Mary Pengelly. I own your cottage. I've got two or three that I let out."

"Well, ours is absolutely beautiful," said Tania. "I'm sure we're going to be very happy there. And thank you for the pack of goodies you left for us."

"The least I could do," said Mary. "We like to make our theatre visitors welcome. After all, they do bring in the trade. So, are you actually in the play?"

"We are," said Ron.

"Well, I'll be seeing a lot of you then," said Mary. "I'm the theatre trust's resident props mistress, so I'll be around to help out." A thought struck her. "Actually, I think I've got some of your friends staying at one of my other cottages. A couple and their daughter. Oh, what's the name now ...?" She flipped her fingers in an effort to remember.

"That'll be Peter and Martha Talbot and Susannah. And their dog, I think."

"That's them. They wanted somewhere dog-friendly, which Wisteria Cottage is."

"Let's hope Hamlet is cottage-friendly," murmured Ron, smiling bravely.

"Hamlet?"

"Peter's Great Dane. He's a bit of a handful sometimes."

"It'll be fine," said Mary carelessly. "Now, I could bring you a menu, but I wouldn't bother with it, actually. You should have the mackerel. It's fresh up from the harbour this teatime. So if that's all right with you ...?" After an exchange of looks, she was rewarded with nods. "And here's me, standing gossiping when there's a bar full of people. I'd better get on, or Toby will have my hide." She bustled away.

*

"That," said Tania, pushing away her plate, "was absolutely superb."

"I loved that gooseberry sauce with it," said Ron.

"Glad you approve," came a rich Cornish burr from a burly man in his sixties as he materialised suddenly at their table. Sharp black eyes twinkled in a weather-beaten face sporting a richly curling black beard, beneath a tousled mane liberally sprinkled with grey. The resemblance to the classical image of a pirate was irresistible. "Oh sorry, didn't mean to make you jump. But that goosegog sauce, that's my wife's idea. She says something about how it cuts the oiliness of the mackerel. But that's all her domain, the kitchen. I leave all that side of things to her." He gathered up the empty plates. "But I'll tell her you enjoyed your meal."

"Please do, Mr ...?"

"Hayle. Tobias Hayle. Call me Toby. I'm the landlord. And I gather from our Mary that you two are with this theatre group that's on next week. I've got some of your lot staying here."

"So we understand," nodded Tania. "Well, I'm sure they won't starve while they're under your roof."

"That they won't," chuckled Toby. "Now, how about puddings? I hope you've left some space, because my missus makes a cracking apple crumble. Comes with local clotted cream. Any chance I can tempt you?"

"Every chance, I should think," smiled Ron. "And I don't think any of my costumes are too tight-fitting," he added in an aside to his wife, "so no danger of a wardrobe malfunction."

"Back in a jiffy," said Toby, and was gone.

Twenty minutes later, Ron sat back with a satisfied sign, and looked up at Toby as he approached their table once more. "Please tell Mrs Hayle," he said, "that that was delicious, and that she is a very talented woman."

Toby chuckled. "Oh, Angela don't need me to tell her. There's plenty others that'll do that, and not just with her cooking. You should see her onstage. Knocks spots off most of them professional actresses, she does. There's those that's told her she ought to have gone on the stage as a career, but she's always been happy doing things just local. But you should'a seen her as Juliet. Marvellous, she was, for all that she was over thirty when she did it. That theatre of ours, it does bring out the best in people."

"We're looking forward to performing there," said Tania.

"Course, you know the story of it?" enquired Toby.

Ron and Tania exchanged glances. "I'm not sure we do," said Ron.

"Ah, well, I got the whole tale from my granddad. He was landlord here before my dad and me. You see, there were these two single ladies come down from London. That was in the 1930s. Bohemian types they were, come down to do some painting. Arty, you might say. Sonia and Sybil Ashton-Rose, their names were. Said they were cousins, and for all we know they might have been, although there were a couple of eyebrows raised, but in those days you didn't like to ask. Anyway, they bought the old cottage where the White House is now, but after a little while they had it knocked down and the new house built there. Rolling in money, they were. Anyway, they used to have some of their arty chums down from London to stay from time to time, and they used to prance about in the gardens doing tableaux and whatnot. Then apparently two of these friends said that the hollow in the cliff reminded them of a Greek theatre, and why didn't they make it into one? Well, that was it. It was goodbye to the paintbrushes and on with the concrete. Took them years, it did, but they ended up with this amazing place. And they named it after these friends of theirs – somebody Mann and somebody Vandyke. Combined the names, see? And the word got around, and theatre folk used to come down from London to put on shows, and it just grew from there. Now we've got our own local dramatic group doing stuff there, plus we have this festival every summer. Woke the whole village up, it did. And half of us are involved, one way or another."

"That's fascinating," marvelled Tania. "I wonder if the others know all that. And we'll certainly have to tell Leah."

"Tell her what?" The question came from a woman who had just burst through the door from the reception area into the bar. She was in her late fifties, of medium height, with a bush of iron-grey hair swept back untidily and with a pair of horn-rimmed glasses perched in the mass, and wearing a camouflage jacket over a pair of dungarees above sturdy lace-up biker boots.

"Leah!" exclaimed Ron and Tania simultaneously. "You made it!"

"Of course," she responded briskly in her robust Scots accent. "And I might have known that the first members of the group I find would be ensconced in the pub. Now, move over, Ron. Let me sit down. I'm gasping for a drink."

"This is Leah Sutherland, our director," explained Ron to Toby, who was looking on with amusement. "Leah, this is Toby Hayle, the landlord."

"And I shall be only too pleased to fetch a drink for you, ma'am," smiled Toby. "What'll you have?"

"Scotch," replied Leah. "Single malt. A triple. I need one."

"Why, what's up?" enquired Tania, concerned, as Toby left on his mission.

"Oh, don't worry about me," said Leah dismissively. "I'm just knackered after having driven that grinding clanking old van I've borrowed for goodness knows how

27

many hours."

"Why, what's wrong with your own car?" asked Ron.

"And how was I supposed to get all the costumes and props into my Jag?" retorted Leah. "It's not a Tardis, you know. So I borrowed a van from an alleged friend. Some friend! It smokes. It rattles. The gearbox is like a bag of spanners. Somebody is going to get an earful when I get back home."

"Well, you're here now," said Tania in soothing tones. "Which is the main thing. In fact, aren't you staying just across the road, over the teashop?"

"You have been doing your homework," replied Leah. "And you're right. And when I got here, I just parked the van, fell out of it, and saw the pub here, so I thought everything else can wait. Ah, thank you, kind sir," she said, as Toby returned and deposited a glass of amber fluid in front of her. "Now, it looks to me as if these two have been filling their faces," she remarked, taking in the empty plates in front of Tania and Ron. "So, mine host, what's good to eat?"

Chapter 3
Saturday

"Smells good," remarked a dressing-gown clad Ron, as he entered the kitchen of Hollyhock Cottage.

"And your entrance is perfectly timed," responded Tania, as she placed two plates of bacon and eggs on the table. "Saturday morning treat. Get that down you. I imagine we've got quite a long day ahead of us."

"Do we know what's happening?" asked Ron, taking a seat and attacking his breakfast with enthusiasm.

"We do. Leah's put out a message to the group this morning. And if you can contain your soul in patience for a few minutes, I'll read it to you. But for the moment, if you don't mind, I'm going to eat my breakfast. If there's one thing I can't abide, it's a congealed fried egg."

"You're the boss," said Ron, and the only sound to be heard for a short while was the clink of cutlery on china as the couple did justice to Tania's cooking.

"More tea?" enquired Ron, as he stood up from the table and placed the breakfast things in the bowl in the kitchen sink. And at Tania's nod, "I'll bung the kettle on, and then I can make it after I've washed up these bits and pieces. And you can tell me what Leah says."

"She's been in touch with the chap who's in charge of the theatre," announced Tania over the sound of running water. "A man by the name of Simeon Ashton-Rose. Apparently he's the grandly titled Artistic Director of the Mandyke Festival Theatre."

"Ashton-Rose? Isn't that the name of the two women who started the theatre in the first place? I'm sure that's what Toby Hayle said."

Tania shrugged. "Obviously some sort of relation. Although probably not a son, if the villagers' suspicions regarding the two ladies were well-founded," she added with a smile. "Not that it's any of our business. Anyway, it seems that there is a building called the Tithe Barn in the grounds of the church, which is available to visiting theatre groups as a rehearsal room. So Leah wants everyone to meet there at ten o'clock this morning, and she can give us all our orders then."

Ron broke off from pouring water into the teapot to look up at the kitchen clock. "That couldn't be better. We can have our tea, and then I can have a shower and a shave while you make yourself look extra beautiful, after which we can saunter down the village and find this barn place."

*

As the couple walked past the Pilchard's Arms, a laughing foursome came tumbling out of the pub's front door.

"Hello, you lot," Ron greeted them. "You seem full of the joys of spring."

"We are," said the leader, a wide-awake looking young man in his early twenties, with dark hair and a friendly look in his eyes. "But I blame the girls. Especially Esther."

"That's not fair, Paul," protested one of the young women, a petite blonde with enormous eyes and a slight giggle in her voice. "It's just as much Sarah's fault. In fact, more so."

"And why's that?" wondered Tania. "What have you been up to, Sarah?"

"Nothing," replied the other girl, taller and a touch sturdier than her friend, and with long straight brown hair. "Just because I said I thought it would be lovely to start off the day with a Buck's Fizz with breakfast, the others didn't have to join in. Especially not with a second bottle of champagne."

"It was only cava," said the second young man, a more serious-looking individual with large owlish glasses and a mop of tousled fair hair. "We're not made of money, you know."

"Timothy's in charge of the joint kitty," explained Paul. "He keeps us all on the straight and narrow."

"So I see," smiled an amused Tania. "But I'd dial back on the alcohol intake if I were you. Leah's not going to be too impressed if you roll up to rehearsal with booze on your breath."

"It was only for this morning," Esther reassured her. "We shall be on our best behaviour for the week, honestly."

"I should hope so," said Tania with mock seriousness. "Tangle with Leah at your peril, as you ought to know by now. Anyway, how did you get on yesterday? Good journey?"

"Fine," said Paul. "I did all the driving, but only because I wanted to arrive in one piece. I mean, have you seen Esther behind the wheel?" He laughed.

"Toad!" riposted Esther, swatting him good-naturedly.

"Funny you should say that," responded Paul, "because your driving has always reminded me of Mr Toad. The only thing we're missing is the 'Poop, poop!'"

"And how's the pub?" enquired Ron, rapidly changing the subject before the warning light in Esther's eyes could develop into anything more serious. "We ate there last night, so we know the food's good. What about the rooms? Sleep well?"

"Not too bad," said Paul. "Apart from the fact that Tim snores. At least, ..." He tried to maintain a straight face, but couldn't manage it. "That's what Sarah tells me," he guffawed.

"Anyway," broke in Tania, clearing her throat meaningfully, "shouldn't we be getting on? We're due at this barn place in a few minutes, and I'm not even quite sure where it is."

"Behind the church, according to Leah's message," said Timothy. "Shouldn't be too hard to find."

As the group approached the lychgate of St. Petroc's church, they encountered a pair of young men in their late teens obviously heading in the same direction.

"Hello, Thomas, hello, James," Ron hailed them. "How was your night under canvas? I see you managed to get yourselves out of bed this morning."

"Don't know what you're talking about, Ron," said the slightly taller of the two. "We've been up for hours. Haven't we, Tom?" He nudged his companion.

"You have," said the other grumpily. "My cousin here," he explained, " was obviously born to live the outdoor life. I think he fancies himself as some sort of Bear Grylls tribute act. Me, I was made for better things. Like proper hot showers, for a start. The shower block at that camp site could do with a bit of sorting out."

"You're a wuss," laughed James. "You should have come for a swim with me first thing. That pool is great. But I might try and find the beach tomorrow morning."

"Cold water swimming?" said Tom with a shudder of horror. "Rescue me from this lunatic, someone," he appealed. "He's mad, you know."

"Have you even had any breakfast?" wondered Tania, concerned.

"Oh, we're fine on that front," James reassured her. "Our tent's right next door to the Kents' van, and Elizabeth did everyone a big fry-up. Even Tom stopped moaning."

"A man's got to keep his strength up," retorted Tom. "Anyway, aren't we supposed to be somewhere?"

"We are," said Tania. "We are summoned by Leah. Better get a move on, or else we'll be in trouble with Herself."

The group made their way into the churchyard, where a substantial stone building could be seen at the far end of the precinct.

*

The Tithe Barn, standing in an even deeper hollow of the church grounds, was a larger structure than it appeared from afar. Evidently of medieval origin, it stone walls were pierced at intervals with tall narrow windows which looked more like arrow-slits than anything, and were thick and sturdy in support of a roof of irregularly-hewn stone slabs. There was a single entrance halfway along one side, with high wide wooden doors such as would have been needed to accommodate the carts which in historical times brought the tribute of parish produce which gave the building its name. The party entered by a smaller wicket let into one of the great doors, to stand momentarily impressed and silenced by the interior. A web of massive rough-hewn oaken timbers, darkened with age, held up the lofty roof, which stretched a full hundred feet in length. At one end was partitioned off a modern interior structure, a two-storey cluster of rooms whose doors bore legends such as 'Props Store' and 'Workshop', with a wooden staircase leading to 'Wardrobe' and doors marked with the symbols for the lavatories. A kitchenette lurked in one corner. At the other end of the barn, a grouping of rostra of different levels was clearly intended to replicate the stage area of the open-air theatre. And in the clear central area stood a cluster of the members of the dramatic society, chatting quietly amongst themselves.

"This is very impressive," remarked Ron to Tania, as their fellows moved past them to greet their friends. "And presumably, as the old saying goes, 'If wet, in church hall'."

"I think you're wrong," replied Tania. "As far as I know, the rule of the theatre is 'The show must go on', so even if it's chucking it down with rain, you still carry on with the performance. It's a matter of honour."

33

Ron pulled a face. "They must breed pretty hardy performers and theatre-goers in this neck of the woods," he observed. "Let's hope the weather holds for us."

"I checked the long-range forecast before we set out yesterday," said Tania. "And the good news is that the BBC says we've got a high-pressure area sitting over us for the next ten days. Clear skies, dry weather, and quite warm days but nippy nights."

"In June? In England?" queried Ron. "Seems unlikely. Do you suppose Leah has been carrying out unholy rites involving black cats and chickens?"

"You," responded Tania, "will get yourself into trouble one of these days." She stepped forward to join the nearest group, a couple in their thirties in the midst of a maelstrom of four small boys. "Good morning, Elizabeth. How are things?"

"How do you think?" smiled the other woman in response, regarding her roistering offspring. "Chaos as usual."

"I've been hearing great things about your catering skills from James and Thomas," said Ron.

"She's had plenty of practice with me," put in the woman's husband alongside her. "I love a Full English. And nothing better for stimulating the appetite than a good dose of country air. And it seemed only fair to feed the troops, seeing as they were camped cheek by jowl with us."

"David has a cunning plan to offload the boys on to James and Tom at some point, so we can catch our breath," said Elizabeth. "James has offered to take them rock-pooling."

"Good luck with that," laughed Tania. "As long as he manages to use up some of their energy so that they're at least halfway controllable in their scene with me."

At that moment, there came the sound of a brisk hand-clap, and Leah, clad in a check lumberjack shirt and her trademark dungarees, stepped up on to a rostrum at the end of the barn. "Now, can you all gather round?" Those present obediently gravitated towards her. "Have we got everybody?"

"The Talbot family aren't here yet," spoke up a serious-looking mature man from the front of the group.

"Typical!" responded Leah. "Late as ever. Thank you, Andrew. Does anyone have any idea where they might be?"

"Right here, Leah," came a voice from the entrance, where a couple in their forties were entering the barn, followed by a pretty girl in her late teens with a pixie-cut hairstyle, who was being towed by an enormous dog. "Sorry if we're a bit late. Hamlet saw a rabbit. Susannah almost lost hold of him, but Martha just caught him in time."

Leah took a breath. "Thank you, Peter. Well, you are here now. So firstly, let me say how pleased and excited I am, and I'm sure you all are too, to have been asked to present our production of 'A Midsummer Night's Dream' here at the Mandyke Theatre. Not everyone gets the chance to appear at this venue, so it's a great feather in our caps. And I'm sure that you're all going to give it your utmost. Now, let me tell you how this is all going to work ..."

"Oh, I think I'm the best person to do that." The interruption, greeted by a fusillade of frenzied barking from Hamlet, came from an individual who had just entered the barn unnoticed, followed by a small group of acolytes. Tall and stick-thin, wearing a cream linen safari suit, he looked to be in his late forties, with a narrow pointy nose and a flop of bleach-blond hair in a style which rightly belonged on a man at least twenty years younger. He strode forward and stepped up alongside Leah.

"Good morning, everyone. My name is Simeon

Ashton-Rose, and I'm the Artistic Director and General Manager of the Mandyke Theatre." The capital letters in the title were clearly audible. "And it's a great pleasure to welcome the members of the ..." He hesitated.

"Ramston," murmured a rather chubbier younger man who had stepped up alongside him.

"The Ramston Dramatic Society," continued Simeon blithely, as if the other had not spoken, "to our wonderful theatre. This is a great honour for you, and I trust you'll make every effort to do us justice."

"We intend to," growled Leah under her breath, tight-lipped.

"So let me tell you what will happen," pressed on Simeon. "Obviously, you will not have access to the theatre until tomorrow, since the current group will be giving their final performance tonight, after which they will be clearing the theatre of all their items in preparation for tomorrow. Incidentally, should any of you wish to watch tonight's show, we do have a few tickets available, and my ... our colleague Matthew Sutcombe here ..." He indicated the young man by his side. "... is box office supervisor, and he would be pleased to organise them for you. Now, you won't know the play, which is brand new, so another triumph for us." He preened – in this context, 'us' was clearly intended to mean 'me'. "The piece is entitled 'Anguish'," he continued, "and is by one of the foremost up-and-coming young authors on the progressive theatre scene. The writing is magnificent, and I cannot recommend it highly enough. It's an intense psychological drama revolving around an orphan with a persecution complex, among many other mental issues, and it's one of the finest pieces of theatre it's ever been my privilege to select for our stage."

"Sound just our cup of tea," muttered Ron to Tania. "Didn't you mention that you were washing your hair tonight?"

"Yes, thank goodness," murmured Tania in reply.

"I may join you."

"But, of course, we have to leaven our offering with more conventional material such as your play, which may be more appealing to the less intellectual audience," Simeon continued, almost succeeding in concealing the faint sneer in his words, as Leah shot him a sideways glare which he completely failed to observe. "Therefore, tomorrow you will be placed in the capable hands of my technical team." He waved a hand vaguely in the direction of his other followers. "Reuben Hawke here is our resident stage manager, and he will be assisted by Ruth Tresillian, his A.S.M." A competent-looking man in his forties raised a hand in acknowledgement, while a mousy girl of around twenty-one bobbed her head shyly. "And the lighting will be in the hands of Naomi Constantine ..." A young woman who looked to be in her late twenties gave a sweet smile. "And no, honestly, she may be a female but she is nevertheless very good at her job, so you need have no worries."

Ron and Tania exchanged looks, eyebrows raised.

"And so, for today, the Tithe Barn is your rehearsal room. Tomorrow, you will have the privilege of setting foot on our hallowed stage. Use your opportunity well." Without waiting for any further reaction, Simeon swept from the room, his box office supervisor trotting in his wake as the rest of his party followed.

*

The somewhat nonplussed silence which followed Simeon's departure was broken by a short bark of mirth from Leah. "Well," she announced to the group, "that's certainly put us in our place." A ripple of amusement ran through the company. "Let's hope the rest of their theatre team don't have the same attitude. What shall we call it? Challenging?"

"Oh, I'm sure they won't," spoke up Tania. "We met their props mistress in the pub last night, and she was as nice as pie."

"Is that the woman who served the breakfasts this morning?" enquired Timothy. "Because she reminded me of my gran."

"No, that was the landlord's wife," Sarah corrected him. "But she was lovely too. Didn't she say that she and her husband organise the bar at the performances."

"And I can vouch for the fact that Toby the landlord is a thoroughly good fellow," said Leah. "At least, he pours a scotch with a very generous hand. So with a bit of luck, we need have no worries." She clapped her hands. "Now, let's get down to some work. I want to do a run-through, chiefly to check that the areas we marked out on the stage at our own theatre work with all these different levels of platforms. And we may as well begin at the beginning.

"So, Theseus and Hippolyta, if you can be standing by offstage right." Ron and Tania moved to the side of the stage area. "And don't forget, we decided last week to scrap the Philostrate lines at the top, and we'll have Egeus do them later in the wedding scene. So carry on straight through, Theseus. And then, we'll have Egeus and the lovers standing by off right. Egeus, you lead." Peter stepped forward. "And then Hermia and Lysander, you follow, hand-in-hand ..." Esther and Paul stepped alongside Peter. "... with Demetrius bringing up the rear." Timothy took up his position. "So, if we're all ready, let's go. Over to you, Ron. '*Now, fair Hippolyta ...*'

Chapter 4
Saturday

"Actually, not bad at all," declared Leah, as a small ripple of applause from around the company ended the brief silence following Susannah's closing speech as Puck. "I think we're in pretty reasonable shape. So I don't propose to keep you too long today. We shall have plenty of hard work to fill our time in the days to come." There was a murmur of surprised approval from the cast, and a general movement to begin collecting belongings together.

"However ..."

A faint sigh of resignation could be detected from all present.

"... there are a couple of things I'd like to spend a moment on, before I actually let you go."

"Do you need all of us?" enquired the wife from the dog-owning couple.

"I do, Martha," replied Leah. "And since you ask, I think we'll start with your first Mechanicals scene. Now, since this is supposed to take place in Peta Quince's house, I know I originally had you all coming on in a group, but I want to change that to take advantage of the playing space we're in. So Martha, since it's your house, you'll be coming through the arch at the back as we planned. You others, I want to scatter around the various entrances we have at our disposal. I've been taking a look at the theatre plan, and I want Bottom to come on from the same entrance as Quince, as if he's in the middle of a conversation with her. And Andrew, cut that line of yours, *'Masters, spread yourselves'*."

"Cut one of Bottom's lines?" laughed Andrew, as he and Martha moved into position. "I don't know if I'm happy about that. He certainly wouldn't be!"

"Theatre is cruel," retorted Leah. "Live with it. Now

next, I want Flute to come on from down right." Thomas moved over to the entrance indicated. "And Starveling, you'll be down left."

"Thank goodness for that," said Elizabeth. "I had a horrible feeling you were going to put me right at the top. And from what I've heard, that seating is awfully steep."

"Call it a fellow-feeling from a middle-aged woman with dodgy knees," smiled Leah. "So Snout, you can have the pleasure of coming down the right-hand side of the precipice in place of your dear wife."

"Art imitating life, then," chuckled David, as he went to stand by, back from the stage front, on the floor of the hall.

"And lastly, Snug, you'll be coming on from the top centre. And if you say your line as you're coming down, you can practice your lion roaring as you arrive at stage level."

"Got it," grinned James. "Prepare for some serious roaring."

"Making sure," intervened Leah severely, "that you don't cover Bottom's lines."

"Fat chance of that," said Andrew. "I'll have his hide if he tries."

"Isn't there some line about a chap who was after a lion's hide and was killed in the hunting of him?" enquired James innocently.

"There will be no lions harmed in the making of this production!" declared Leah in determined tones. "So, carry on. Let's make this work, since I presume you don't want to spend all day here."

*

"That was good," said Leah. There were faint but unmistakeable sighs of relief. "The only thing the Pyramus and Thisby scene now needs is an audience. So don't take it up any further, or it'll be over the top. And by the way ... well roared, Lion." As James seemed to be

40

stricken with an uncharacteristic blush at the unexpected praise, Leah considered for a moment. "Right. Just one or two small bits and pieces with the Immortals, and then we can call it a day. By the way, well done, Daniel, for keeping going when Susannah lost her lines for the moment in your first scene together. And remember, Susannah, Puck is going to call Daniel 'Spirit' all through that scene, rather than 'Fairy'."

"Can't she just call me 'Moth'?" piped up the seven-year-old. "That is my name."

"Ah, but we don't know that yet," explained Leah. "Not until your scene with Bottom."

"Sorry, Leah. I forgot about the change," confessed Susannah. "Do you want us to do it again?"

"No, I'm sure you'll remember next time. So that's it for you. But I still need Daniel, because I want ..." The rest of her words were drowned out by a deafening burst of barking from Hamlet. "Peter!" Leah thundered. "Can you not keep that hell-hound of yours under control? Need I remind you, we are not doing 'Julius Caesar'? I do not require you to let slip the dogs of war!"

"Sorry again," apologised the dog's owner. "But you did say you wanted a big dog for the hunting scene."

"Hmmm," grunted Leah. "Don't make me regret that. And I would dearly have loved a real Talbot, if only the breed weren't extinct. So you can tell Hamlet to behave himself, or else he may be joining their numbers."

"It's just that ... well, there's a butterfly in here," explained Peter, "and it almost landed on Hamlet's nose."

Susannah sprang forward. "Here, Dad. Let me take him outside out of the way." She gathered up the leash of the Great Dane, which was still straining to reach the insect which had fluttered up into the barn's rafters.

"I'll come with you." Ron stepped forwards. "We can go through our lines in the 'I know a bank' bit. I still almost fell over the 'woodbine' and 'eglantine' section."

The pair exited towards the churchyard.

"And now," said Leah, after taking a very deep breath, "as I was saying, I just want to do the scene with Bottom and the four fairies. So Daniel, if you would like to round your brothers up ..." With a smile befitting one whose lofty one-year's advantage over his siblings placed him in an unrivalled position of command, Daniel dashed away to a far corner of the barn, where the six-year-old triplets were engaged in a surprisingly quiet game among themselves. "And we'll start from just after Quince's exit, so Bottom, it's your line 'I see their knavery ...'"

"Have we got my ass's head here?" enquired Andrew, as he stepped up on to the acting area. "Because I'm worried that I may still be too muffled."

"Don't fret," came the reply. "It's all been modified, and I've got it in my van with the rest of the costumes and props. You shall have it tomorrow when we're at the theatre, and then we can be absolutely sure that the back row of seats will be able to receive the full blast of your not-so-dulcet tones. Now, boys." Leah softened her voice and turned to the three youngest members of the cast, lined up expectantly before her. "It was a wee bit of a muddle when you came on before, because you all tried to enter at once, and I don't think there will be room through the arch. So, all you need to do is listen for when the Fairy Queen calls your name, and on you come. So Josh, that's you first as Peaseblossom, followed by Noah as Cobweb. Daniel, can you give them each a gentle shove at the appropriate moment?" A nod from the senior brother, bursting with pride at the importance of his rôle. "And you both come to the right of Bottom, and then it's Daniel himself, and lastly Zak as Mustardseed on the left. Now, Tania, if you'd like to drape yourself alluringly on this rather unyielding rostrum, which I promise you will have a pile of cushions, once we've unloaded the van, and off we go."

*

"So, how are you feeling, Ron?" asked Tania, as the couple walked up through the churchyard to the fading sound of jangling keys, as Leah locked up the door of the Tithe Barn behind them.

"Hungry," replied Ron.

Tania laughed. "I mean about the play, idiot! How do you think it went this morning?"

"Oh, that." Ron considered. "Actually, I think it went pretty well. I mean, it's the first time we've run through it off home turf, so it was bound to be a bit rough round the edges, but it was helpful to get a sense of the area we'll be playing in. That ought to make it easier when we get on to the actual stage tomorrow. Mind you, it'll be completely different when we're doing it in the open air."

"True," agreed Tania. "In fact, that's the one thing I'd be fretting about if I were Leah."

"And what would be troubling you if you were me?" came the sudden deep voice of the director as she came up behind the pair.

"Oh, sorry, Leah," said Tania, startled. "Didn't see you there."

"So what fresh problem have you devised for me, among the goodness-knows-how-many I shall be contending with when we get to the theatre?" Leah pressed her.

"Oh, just audibility," explained Tania. "I mean, some of the kids aren't used to projecting that much ..."

Leah chuckled. "Are you sure? I've heard the racket David and Elizabeth's boys can make when they're playing together at the start of rehearsals. Deafening! Hearing them is going to be the least of my worries."

"And then there's Andrew. He was telling me he's still concerned about being heard when he's wearing the

43

ass's head."

"And I've already told him, there's no problem. The mask has been modified so that there's no covering whatsoever for his mouth." Leah sighed. "I'll make a point of showing him when we're at the theatre tomorrow. But in any event, from what I've been assured, being heard is going to be the last thing anyone has to concern themselves with. I had a chat with the director of one of last year's productions, and he told me that the acoustics are excellent. Apparently the whole place has been designed on the model of a Greek theatre, so you will all be heard perfectly. So if Andrew is determined to whinge, I shall be forced to deliver a smart kick up the Bottom!" A bark of mirth.

"So do we know the arrangements for tomorrow?" enquired Ron.

"Not yet. But I should know fairly soon. Just as I was locking up, I got a text from that stage manager fellow. He wants a chat, so he suggested I call on him in his shop this afternoon."

"Of course!" exclaimed Ron. "That artistic director chap said the stage manager was a guy called Hawke, and that's the name of that ironmonger's shop in the main street, isn't it?"

"Well remembered, Ron," said Tania admiringly. "And if you think about it, who better for a stage manager than somebody local with all the tools and hardware at his fingertips?"

"Well, I shall see what he's got for me, and then I'll message everybody to let them know the plan," said Leah.

"Do you mind if we tag along?" asked Ron. "The shop's only just up here next to the place you're staying, and we're heading that way anyway, so I'd like to know what's in store. I've got a feeling tomorrow's going to be a long day."

"More than likely," agreed Leah. "So yes, by all means. You may think of some questions that don't occur to me."

"And then," said Tania, "I think we'll probably go and grab some lunch in the pub. Ron was just complaining of hunger pangs, and I know he had a hankering for a pint and a pasty. Why don't you join us?"

"Well ... if you're sure you don't mind?" An unexpected hint of shyness was evident in Leah's question. "I mean, I know some of our people are a bit wary of me ..."

"Of course not," returned Tania robustly. "And it's not as if we can be accused of trying to cosy up to the director, is it? I mean, we've already got the parts." She laughed.

"Well, in that case, the first drink's on me," said Leah, a smile lighting up her sometimes severe features. "And now, here we are." She pushed open the door of Hawke's Hardware.

The odour that greeted the three as they entered was a warm and not unpleasant mixture of paraffin and polish, fertiliser and fire-lighters, paint and putty. "Wow," said Ron. "That takes me back. I haven't smelt that smell since I was a kid."

"How do you mean?" wondered Tania.

A nostalgic look came over Ron's face. "There was a little row of shops up the road from where we used to live. One of them was an old-fashioned family ironmonger's, run by this old chap in a long brown warehouse coat. He seemed about a hundred to me, but then I was only around ten, so he was probably only middle-aged. Mind you, I don't expect the shop had changed since his grandfather ran it during the war. Fricker's Utilities, the place was called. And whatever you wanted, whether it was an odd-sized screw, or a new handle for an old broom, or a packet of cup-hooks, or some creosote for the garden fence ..."

"Or four candles?" put in Tania, a mischievous glint in her eye.

"Laugh all you want," retorted Ron with a rueful smile. "But that shop was the smell of my childhood. That's where you'd go for anything and everything. I used to go in there to buy glue when I'd run out of it for my model plane kits. And now, suddenly, I feel like a kid again."

Tania put her arm through her husband's and deposited a fond kiss on his cheek. "You'll always be a kid to me, darling," she smiled.

At that moment, a man appeared from the rear of the shop. He carried an axe in his hand, and there was a frown on his face. "Sorry, I didn't realise anyone had come in. Has that blasted doorbell of mine gone on the blink again?"

Leah stepped forward. "It *is* Mr Hawke, isn't it? I don't know if you remember us. We're from the Ramston drama group."

The man's brow cleared. "Of course. We met earlier on down at the Barn, although rather briefly, I'm afraid." He caught his visitors looking askance at the axe in his hand, and laughed. "Oh, don't worry. This isn't normally the way I greet visitors to the shop. I was just sharpening it for one of my customers. So, let's do the introductions properly. The name's Reuben Hawke." He set the axe aside and extended a hand in greeting.

"And I'm Leah Sutherland," replied Leah, taking the hand. "I'm the director of our production of 'Dream', and these two are Tania and Ron Faye. They're playing our two leads."

"Is that the two leads or all four?" enquired Reuben. "Theseus and Hippolyta as well as the Fairy Queen and King?" He was answered with nods. "Thought as much. Most people do it that way. Better, I reckon. I love that play," he explained. "It was the first one I ever did when I was at school. In fact, there are people in the village who still speak with admiration of my Bottom," he added, a grin splitting his rugged good looks. "Sorry, terrible old gag which I expect you've all heard a million times. But the point is, I know the whole thing backwards. But my acting days are long over. I'm much happier working behind the scenes these days, so I'm really looking forward to helping with your production."

"That's actually what I wanted a word about," said Leah. "I need to know what are the arrangements for tomorrow, so I can notify my cast."

"Oh, that's easy," said Reuben. "My team and I will be down at the theatre tonight to help the current lot break down and clear out, but with luck that won't take too long. It's a pretty simple thing – they've just got one bed and a doorway. Will any of your company be going to see the play tonight?"

"Well ..." came the evasive reply from Tania.

Reuben laughed. "I can't say I blame you. It's a miserable piece, and I don't suppose you were particularly enticed by Simeon's description of it earlier on, so I don't reckon you'll be missing much. He's got some odd ideas at the best of times, has our Simeon, but maybe we oughtn't to go down that road just now. No, you'd best get yourselves an early night, because there'll be plenty to do tomorrow. And as for timing, we'll all be reassembling out front of the White House for ten o'clock sharp, so if you can tell your people to be there ready and waiting for then, that'll be perfect. I can give everybody the conducted tour, go through all the safety stuff, and we can get cracking."

"What about access? I've got a van full of costumes and props parked out here. What's the best way of getting those to the theatre?" enquired Leah.

"Oh, that's your van, is it?"

47

"Don't ask." Leah shuddered. "Borrowed for the occasion, and I shall be only too glad to see the back of it after the production. That's if it makes it all the way back to Ramston," she added.

"Well, there's no problem," said Reuben. "There's a little road going down from the side of the White House which leads down to the side of the stage. Park out front, and I'll show you. It's a bit steep, so I hope that van's got good brakes. And you can unload there, save carting everything down through the house itself. You'll be able to steer well clear of Simeon's domain."

"That sounds perfect," said Leah. "Apart from the costumes, there's just a mossy bank, a couple of thrones, a box of props, and a whole pile of cushions. I'll enlist the youngsters to help. Thank you, Reuben." She shook the stage manager's hand once more. "I'll let everyone know, and we'll see you tomorrow. And now," she added, as the three left the hardware shop, "let me see if I can make good on that promise of mine." She chuckled. "I wonder why it is that, after a rehearsal, the members of the Ramston Players so often end up in the pub?" She stepped out across Fore Street.

Chapter 5
Saturday

"Do we do pasties?" Tobias Hayle let out an exuberant roar of laughter, which echoed round the bar of the Pilchard's Arms. "Here, Angela," he called to a dumpy apron-clad woman standing at the far end of the bar, two bottles of beer in her hands. "Gentleman here wants to know if we do pasties." The enquiry provoked a small rustle of laughter from the scatter of patrons around the room.

"We better," replied the woman with a smile, "else I'm going to have to drink these myself instead of putting them in my beef and stout mix. Which is just bubbling along nicely, so if you'll excuse me, I'll be getting back to my kitchen." She disappeared through a door at the rear of the bar.

"I'm taking it the answer is yes," ventured Ron. "And you can't really blame me for asking, because we never got to see your menu when we were in last night. Not that we're complaining. Your barmaid's recommendation was perfect."

"Ah, well, our Mary do know about food. But then she would, coming from that family."

"Sorry?" Tania was puzzled. "What family?"

"Of course, you wouldn't know," said Toby. "Her sister Judith owns the cafe just across Fore Street from here."

"Oh, we noticed it yesterday. I promised myself a cream tea there."

"Well, you won't be disappointed," nodded Toby. "Which you will be, if I don't sort you out some food. Now, here's that menu you were after."

"You two go and sit yourselves down," suggested Leah. "And I'll get those drinks I promised you."

*

49

"That," said Ron, laying down his knife and fork, "was the best pasty I've ever had."

"They were pretty good," agreed Tania. "You probably won't want to eat anything else for the rest of the day."

"Don't you believe it," scoffed Ron. "What we need is a good bracing walk in the fresh Cornish air, and then we'll be all set up for that cream tea you fancied. And then we won't have to bother with cooking anything this evening."

"That does actually sound quite an attractive idea," smiled Tania.

"Plus," intervened Leah, wiping an errant crumb from alongside her mouth, "depending on how tomorrow goes, you might not have the chance to go out for tea. We could hit some snags and be stuck at the theatre until goodness knows what time."

"Good thought," said Ron.

"Well, ladies and gent, how were the pasties?" enquired Toby, materialising alongside their table once again with his faint air of a Gilbertian pirate king. "I hope they lived up to your expectations."

"Even more so," said Ron. "I think I'm beginning to get attracted to the Cornish life."

"You wouldn't be the first," chuckled Toby. "And you were very wise to choose the classic beef and veg recipe. That's based on what the old tin miners used to have for their snap. It's definitely our most popular. They're even better than the ones Tresillian sells in his shop, and they've won prizes at the County Show. But maybe next time, you might try Angela's pork and apple pasty. That one always goes down well, for all that it's a bit Somerset for my taste. So anyway, can I get you anything else?"

"I don't think so," said Ron, a slight note of regret audible in his voice. "Not that I couldn't easily fancy another one of your wife's puddings, but we're going to take a walk to shake down lunch so that we've got room for a cream tea at the cafe."

"Right you are." Toby moved away.

"I'm still worried about all that food we've brought with us," fretted Tania. "We've got a freezer full, and it's got to be eaten some time."

"Problem?" asked Leah.

Tania pulled a face. "Well, a bit of one. You see, we'd planned to ask everybody back to our place after the play on opening night for a bit of a party. You know, either to celebrate our great success or, heaven forbid, drown our sorrows if it's all gone wrong. Which I'm sure it won't, Leah," she added hastily.

"That sounds a delightful idea," said Leah. "So what's worrying you?"

"We didn't realise the cottage would be quite so ... cosy," explained Ron, glancing warily in the direction of the bar, where Mary could be seen polishing glasses, and not wishing to offend her. "And I don't think we could fit everyone in, especially if we invite some of the local stage crew along as well. So we've got all this party food, and we're not quite sure what to do with it."

"Sorry, couldn't help overhearing," intervened Toby, popping back from the neighbouring table where he had been collecting plates and glasses. "Do I gather you're wanting somewhere to have your first night after-show party?"

"That's right," said Ron.

"Then that's easy," smiled Toby. "Have it here."

"Here?" echoed Tania. "How ... I mean where? I'm sure you can't be expected to set up for us here in your bar when you've got a pub to run and everything."

"No need," said Toby. "You can use our ballroom."

"You have a ballroom?" wondered Leah, surprised.

"Oh, just a small one. It's up on the first floor. The

51

Assembly Room, they used to call it in Georgian times when this place was built. We were quite the hub of local society in those days, so they used to have a ball here every so often. These days we mostly use it for wedding receptions and such. Why don't you come and have a look?"

"We'd love to," said Tania, rising from her seat with the light of hope in her eyes, as Ron followed suit.

"You two carry on," said Leah. "I'm off to put my feet up for a while. I think I'm going to need to husband all my reserves for tomorrow, and I've got to let everyone know about the plans for the morning. So I shall see you anon." With a smile and a nod, she made her way out of the bar.

"Keep an eye, would you, Mary?" called Toby to his bar colleague. "I'm just popping up to the ballroom a second." At the top of the hall staircase, he threw open a pair of impressive carved doors to reveal a large room lined with wooden panelling beneath a plaster ceiling decorated with swags of foliage and cherubs, above a line of glittering chandeliers. Light from three tall sash windows flooded the room. "There," he announced proudly. "That's our ballroom. They do say that Jane Austen danced here one time. Will it do?"

"Do?" gasped Tania, entranced. "It's beautiful. But are you sure? I mean, we wouldn't want to put anyone to any trouble."

"No trouble at all," Toby assured her. "And as for food, don't give it a second thought. You can add your stuff to whatever's left over from the Midsummer Mumming."

"What's the Midsummer Mumming?" asked Ron, puzzled.

"Bless me, don't you know?" said Toby, scratching his beard in amazement. "I'd have thought that was why you chose your play, because it was this particular week."

"Sorry, I don't understand."

"On account of the summer solstice," explained the landlord. "Which as you know is on the twenty-first of June, which is the first night of your play, isn't it? And on that day, there's a village celebration in honour of the season."

"Oh, I see," said Ron, light beginning to dawn. "Like the Floral Dance they have in Helston."

"I think you mean the Furry Dance," Toby corrected him. "That Terry Wogan has a lot to answer for," he muttered.

"So what happens?" asked Tania. "Is it one of those old pagan rituals? Or medieval?"

Toby chuckled. "Yes and no. You see, there was this old tradition of a midsummer celebration in the village in the middle ages, but it died out years ago. Probably killed off by the Puritans, I expect. They never wanted anyone to have a good time. But then the ladies at the White House, Miss Sonia and Miss Sybil, they got to hear of it somehow, and they determined to revive it. It was probably just a chance for their fancy London chums to prance about in costumes to start with, but all of a sudden, it took off. The village thought it put them on the map. So they started up a dance troupe ..."

"What, Morris dancing?"

"Ah, no. According to Miss Sybil, it was properly called 'Moorish' dancing, on account of it came from Africa originally. And they used to have blackened faces, but of course, we don't do that no more. Anyway, the ladies worked out this whole procedure. It all starts off with a feast on Midsummer's Eve – that's what goes on here. Everyone comes, and the lads in the village compete to see who's the strongest and best-looking and what-have-you, and then the villagers choose the two who are the best, and the actual winner gets to represent the spirit of Midsummer, and he gets to lead the procession."

"Is that what they call the "'Obby 'Oss'?" wondered Tania.

"Certainly not!" replied Toby with mock severity. "The 'Obby 'Oss is what they have in Padstow. That's North Cornwall. We got much better down here. We have the 'Obby Ass."

Tania laughed. "Well, I've never heard of that. What is it?"

"Isn't it obvious?" said Ron. "It's a donkey version of the horse."

"Pretty much," admitted Toby. "Our chap has a big cape made of straw woven with ribbons, and on his head he wears a straw mask in the shape of the donkey."

"You don't suppose that's where Shakespeare got the idea for the bit in our play, do you?" surmised Tania.

Toby shrugged. "Couldn't say. So anyway, on Midsummer Morn, they're all supposed to get up at dawn, not that anybody does these days. First of all, the fiddler strikes up. That's worth getting up early for by itself. If you ain't heard old Ezekiel Tregorrick on his fiddle, you ain't heard nothing. There's nobody can squeeze out a tune on that thing like him, for all that he's eighty-odd. We have him here to play in the bar sometimes. And then the Moorish dancers process through the village, led by the 'Obby Ass and the lad who came runner-up, who gets to be the Lord of Misrule. He's the one who's in charge of the Ass's Carrot."

Ron and Tania exploded in mirth. "The Ass's Carrot?" gasped Tania. "What's that all about?"

"It's all perfectly serious," said Toby, who seemed to be having his own problems keeping a straight face. "The 'Obby Ass has an official carrot. It's called the Carrot of Love. And the village maidens ... now don't laugh, cos we still got a few ... they come to their front gates as the procession goes by, and they have to kiss the Ass's carrot

54

..."

"Stop it, stop it!" pleaded Tania, now almost helpless with laughter.

"I do hope that's not some kind of euphemism," Ron managed to gurgle.

"And any maiden chosen by the Ass," continued Toby manfully, "is guaranteed to find her own true love within a twelvemonth."

"And this happens every year?" Tania managed to regain her breath. "And it's happening this week?"

"That's right," confirmed Toby. "And it brings a lot of tourists into the village. Very good for trade, it is. And I dare say it'll do your ticket sales no harm at all. Loads of people stay on for the evening if there's a good play on. And I can't help thinking yours is perfect. So anyway, what do you say about the room?"

"It couldn't be better," smiled Tania. "Thank you so much, Toby."

"And as for food, as I say, there's bound to be plenty left over after the Midsummer's Eve feast, so Angela would be only too pleased for you people to have it for your after-show party."

"Then it's a deal," said Ron, shaking Toby's hand.

"And there's plenty of room," continued Tania enthusiastically, "so that we can invite everybody who's anything to do with the play. Not just the cast – we can have all the crew, and the management too. We'll be one big happy family."

The landlord raised an eyebrow. "Management too? Are you sure?"

"Of course. Why not?"

"Well, I'm sure you know best." Toby forbore to comment further.

"And I wouldn't mind betting," added Ron, "that our cast will have developed a thirst during the evening. You may even end up taking a few quid at the bar."

"Well, that thought never crossed my mind," twinkled Toby. "So then everyone's happy."

*

Tania sighed. "I could live here."

"You reckon?" queried Ron, as he leaned back on the bench which the couple occupied on the clifftop overlooking Polkernow Bay.

"It's idyllic," replied his wife as, eyes closed, she let the westering sun, declining now from its noon brilliance but still with the warm glow of a late summer's afternoon, bathe her face in gold.

The couple had strolled without any particular aim in mind, passing through the village with its whitewashed slate-roofed cottages, interspersed with an occasional more modern bungalow whose impeccably groomed garden with its geometrically precise flower borders spoke of elderly retired occupants. They clambered over a stile, where the faded legend 'Public footpath' could just be discerned on the weather-beaten finger-post leaning wearily for support against the adjacent dry stone wall. The path, the tall unkempt grass and wild flowers at its margins alive with mysterious rustlings which suddenly stilled as the pair passed, took them between high hedges from which small birds unexpectedly erupted, emerging into an area of grass and gorse which ran along the top of the cliff, eventually vanishing into a steep tree-lined cleft which appeared to lead down to a tiny pebbly cove below.

"That's as may be," said Ron. "It may be wonderful on a sunny summer's afternoon like this, but I bet it'd be a different story sitting here on a winter's day with a gale howling in off the Atlantic. You do know there's nothing between here and America, don't you?"

Tania sat up and batted him affectionately. "Spoilsport!"

"And then there's the shops. I don't offhand know

56

where the nearest supermarket is, but I bet it's not just five minutes away. And what about those Saturday mornings when you fancy just nipping into town and wandering round the shops looking for nothing in particular, and then maybe meeting up with the girls from R.O.A.D.S. for a coffee?"

"You, Mr Faye," announced Tania haughtily, sitting up and gazing out to sea, "have, I have decided, been misnamed. 'Ron' is entirely unsuitable for you. From now on, you shall be known as 'Eeyore'."

Ron put his arm around his wife and drew her to him, depositing a kiss on her cheek. "Just being practical, love. For one thing, I doubt if there are many job openings for management consultants around these parts. So how am I going to keep you in the style to which you have become accustomed?"

"We could keep chickens and grow our own vegetables," smiled Tania, ruefully relenting. "Or take in washing? Maybe open our own tin mine?" laughingly suggested Ron. "I know it may be the dream to get out of town and lead the simple life, but it's probably not for everyone. However," he said, as Tania seemed about to object, "there are considerable advantages to living somewhere like this. For instance ..." He paused tantalisingly. "I bet that in Ramston you don't stand a snowball's chance of getting a genuine Cornish cream tea. Whereas here ..."

"Beast!" retorted Tania. "You always know how to get round me."

"So do you reckon you've managed to work up sufficient appetite to handle whatever they have on offer at the village teashop?"

Tania jumped to her feet and seized Ron by the hand. "Now you're talking. And to make up for being such a misery, you can treat me."

Ron sighed as he stood. "Hands up, anyone who's

surprised."

*

The bell above the door of 'A Cake and a Cuppa' tinkled resoundingly as Ron ushered Tania into the teashop's cosy interior.

A cheerful-looking middle-aged woman wearing a frilly flowered apron emerged from behind the counter to greet her visitors. "Good afternoon, my loves. Afternoon tea, is it?"

Tania looked around the room, where only one table was occupied, and that by a couple who seemed in the throes of preparing to leave. "That's if we're not too late."

The woman smiled. "Bless you, my love. Of course you're not. We don't close for another half hour yet, so you've plenty of time. And I won't throw you out if you go over by a few minutes," she dimpled. "So you sit yourselves down – there, that table in the window is the best, and I'll be over to take your order in just a jiffy." She occupied herself with seeing her other customers off the premises, amidst much smiling and nodding and declarations of intent to return, before making her way over to where Tania and Ron had installed themselves. "So, what'll it be?"

"I think we'd like a cream tea for two, please," said Ron.

"Ah, but which sort?" enquired the woman. "There's the Duchess's Tea, which is finger sandwiches, a plain scone with jam and cream, and a slice of cake. And a pot of tea, of course. Or we've got the specials, but those are mostly for the children."

"I'm feeling like a child on a birthday treat," declared Tania. "So do tell us."

"Well, there's Teddy's Tea, for a start. That comes with a honey scone and an orange and honey tea-loaf. Then you've got Tufty's Tea ..."

58

"Is that named after Tufty the squirrel?" wondered Ron. "Because I remember him from when I was a kid. Something to do with road safety, wasn't he?"

"That's right. And that's with a hazelnut scone and a coffee-and-walnut cake. And lastly, we've got Bunny's Tea ..."

"Don't tell me - carrot cake!" said Tania.

"That's right," beamed the cafe-owner. "And a wholemeal fruit scone to go with it. And of course, you've got your tea and sandwiches as well. Although, for the children, there's squash, and with Bunny's Tea there's the option of a glass of Dandelion and Burdock"

"Sounds like a feast," said Ron. "Darling ...?"

"You know I do love a nice carrot cake," replied Tania. "But I think I'll stick with a pot of tea."

"So, one Tufty's Tea for me, please, and one Bunny's Tea for my wife." Ron tried to stop himself giggling, as the woman bustled into the kitchen at the back.

Chapter 6
Saturday

"And there's your carrot cake." A plate with a gigantic slice of moist-looking gateau, filled and topped with a generous layer of buttercream and adorned with tiny orange fondant carrots, was placed in front of Tania, while Ron received an equally impressive portion of coffee-and-walnut cake.

"Good grief! These are enormous!" exclaimed a beaming Ron. "I may not need to eat anything else for a week." He picked up a fork.

"We do like to look after our customers," smiled the teashop owner comfortably. "Especially the ones who've come down to do a play for us."

"Oh dear. Are we that obviously theatrical?" wondered Tania.

"Not at all, my love. It's just that we can usually tell."

"That's funny. That's what the barmaid in the pub said."

"Our Mary? Oh, there isn't much that gets past her."

"Your Mary ...? You mean the woman we're renting our cottage from?"

"That's right, my love. I'm her sister Judith. Judith Polkerris."

"Well, it's a pleasure to meet you, Mrs Polkerris," said Ron, pausing to wipe cake crumbs from around his mouth. "Sorry, it is 'Mrs', is it?"

"It certainly is. Married to my Ben these thirty-one years."

"And does he work in the teashop with you?" asked Tania. "Surely you don't run the place all on your own?"

"Bless you, no. I do all the baking myself, and Mary helps out, and I got some of the girls from the village working here as waitresses, but I sent this afternoon's girl off early at four o'clock because she had a birthday party for one of her daughter's school-friends to go to." It seemed that Judith's definition of 'girl' was somewhat elastic. "And as for my Ben," she continued, chuckling, "I can't really see him looking right in one of our pinnies. I don't think it'd go with his uniform."

"Uniform?"

"He's the village bobby," explained Judith. "We got the police house a few doors along. That's how come I let out the upstairs flat here for visitors. In fact, there's one of your ladies staying there this week, isn't there?"

"That's right," said Tania. "Our director Leah."

"I met her when she arrived. Nice woman. A bit brusque though."

"Oh, that's just her way. She's actually very pleasant when you get to know her. But I suspect she cultivates the gruff image deliberately in order to keep some of our naughtier cast members under control," chuckled Tania. She nudged her husband. "Specially this one."

"I should think your husband's got a pretty charmed life, living somewhere like this," suggested Ron airily, affecting not to notice his wife's remark. "I can't imagine that you'd be troubled with much in the way of serious crime around here. Judging by the people we've met so far, like your sister and the pub landlord, the whole village seems like one big happy family."

There was an odd pause. "Oh, my Ben gets plenty to do," said Judith. "You'd be surprised. There's folks coming in from up-country and stealing tractors and suchlike, or else you get visitors' dogs running wild in amongst the livestock, and then Ben has to go out and pacify the farmers and persuade them to put their shotguns back in their cabinets where they rightly belong, and of course there's always going to be the problem with the parking ..." She stopped abruptly.

61

"Parking?" enquired Tania delicately after a moment.

"Oh, I ought not to gossip," said Judith with a slightly strained smile. "It's not as if it's anything to worry yourselves about. Although ..."

Tania pulled across a chair from the adjacent table and patted the seat invitingly. "Now," she coaxed, with an encouraging smile, "if there's one thing I enjoy, it's a bit of gossip. And since we're going to be around for the next week, we might as well have a little bit of the local dirt. And it's not as if we're in a particular hurry. So ..."

Judith seated herself in the proffered chair with a sigh. "I suppose you might as well know. After all, it might affect you, what with the play and all. And of course, we've got the Mumming as well, which won't help."

"So what's the problem?" wondered Ron.

Judith took a deep breath. "It's that Simeon."

"What, Simeon Ashton-Rose? The director of the theatre?"

"That's the one," replied Judith grimly. "He's the only Simeon we've got. And one too many, if you ask me."

"We did actually meet him," said Tania. "Well, that's not strictly true. It wasn't exactly a social occasion. He came to our rehearsal this morning at the barn to introduce himself and some of the theatre's people."

"Ah well, then you'll have had a taste of what he's like. Full of himself, and as rude as you please. Lord knows what the village ever did to deserve him. But apparently he's some sort of nephew of the old ladies who built the theatre, so when the last of them popped off a few years back, the theatre trust saw fit to appoint him, and he's been here ever since. He lives in the White House, and he seems to think that makes him some kind of lord of the manor."

"So what's all this about parking?" asked Ron.

"There's a big car park up the west end of the village, near the caravan park," explained Judith. "I expect you've seen it."

"We haven't been up that far," said Tania. "Our cottage is at the other end."

"It's supposed to be for visitors to leave their cars so they can walk into the village proper," continued Judith. "And there's a set of steps going down from there to the harbour. Trouble is, most tourists just park their cars at the side of the roads, specially people coming to the theatre, and Simeon is always complaining to Ben that he ought to keep the traffic under control and make people obey the rules. And what makes him specially hot under the collar is when they park on the grass at the front of the White House and block up his access. Hopping mad, he gets, and he says that Ben don't give two figs for him, and a couple of times he's threatened to go to the Chief Constable and put in a formal complaint about Ben's incompetence so that he can get him sacked."

"That does seem rather over the top," said Ron.

"Well, that just what he's like," said Judith. "Course, he's never forgiven my Ben for booking him for speeding when he first came to the village. And it weren't as if it was just the odd mile-an-hour or two either. A right old Jehu, Ben said."

"Jehu?" queried Tania.

"You know, like that chap in the Bible," explained Judith. "There's some bit about somebody called Jehu, who 'driveth furiously', apparently. Can't you tell Ben went to Sunday School when he was a kid?" She smiled indulgently, but then her expression became solemn once more. "And my Ben's not the only one who's felt the rough edge of Simeon's tongue, from what I've heard. I'm sure there's many round here who could tell a tale." She suddenly seemed to realise that she had perhaps said too much to a pair of total strangers. "But here, you don't want me telling you all our woes, when you've just come in here for a nice relaxing tea." She stood.

"And that's exactly what it was," Tania reassured her. "Delicious." She looked at her watch and got to her feet. "And here we've been keeping you talking, and I'm sure it's long past your closing time. So Ron, please pay the lady, and we'll get out of her way. And I'm sure we'll be back, and I'll make sure we tell all the others how wonderful this place is."

*

"We got a little more than we bargained for at 'A Cake and a Cuppa', didn't we?" remarked Tania, as the couple walked hand-in-hand up Fore Street in the direction of Hollyhock Cottage.

"Or should we now think of it as 'A Cake and a Copper'?" quipped Ron. "But it was certainly instructive," he mused. "Do you suppose 'A Cake and a Cuppa' is the epicentre of all the local news?"

"I shouldn't be surprised. The people round here do seem to have a habit of speaking freely. Not like us townies, all buttoned-up and repressed. Mind you, what you said about all the locals being one big happy family seems a bit wide of the mark."

"I don't know about that," said Ron. "The only person we've heard a bad word about so far is that Simeon What's-his-face chap. And to be frank, going from his first appearance at rehearsal this morning, it sounds as if we might be justified in judging that particular book by its cover."

"Well, with a bit of luck, we won't need to have anything to do with him," said Tania. "After all, I can't see why he would need to be involved with our play when he seems to have a whole lot of minions at his command."

"Let's hope that's the case." Ron looked up the road ahead of the pair and nudged his wife. "And speak of the devil. Look who's coming down the road."

Ron was not mistaken. Stalking towards them down Fore Street with long strides, his head aloft, came Simeon Ashton-Rose, his companion from the morning scuttling along a pace behind him in an attempt to keep up, while his efforts seemed constantly frustrated by the diminutive white Bichon Frisé he held on a lead, whose intention seemed to be to stop at every enticing gatepost and tuffet for prolonged sniffing.

"Well, here's a chance to find out for ourselves," murmured Tania, as she switched on her friendliest smile. "Good afternoon, Mr Ashton-Rose," she hailed the approaching theatre manager.

At her words, the small white dog let out a torrent of high-pitched yaps, which were eventually stilled by his handler. "Sorry," muttered the young man, embarrassed. "She always does that with people she's not used to."

Simeon looked faintly taken aback to be addressed by Tania. "Sorry, do we know each other?" he enquired, looking down the long promontory that was his nose.

"Oh, I'm not at all surprised you don't remember us." Tania gave a gentle self-deprecating laugh, as her husband regarded her with a sideways look. "There were so many of us at the rehearsal room this morning, and I'm sure you must have had a great deal too much on your mind to notice us individually. We're in the cast of Ramston's 'Midsummer Night's Dream'. I'm Tania Faye, and this is my husband Ron." She held out a hand, which Simeon reluctantly took. "But please call me Tania. And it's Simeon, isn't it?"

"Er ... that's correct." And in response to Tania's enquiring look, eyebrows expectantly raised, in the direction of his companion, "This is Matthew Sutcombe."

"Of course," responded Tania warmly. "I remember you introduced him this morning. Hello, Matthew." She again extended her hand, to be greeted by a tentative handshake and a shy mumble. "You're in charge of the box office at the theatre, aren't you? I hope you've managed to sell lots of tickets for our play," she continued brightly.

"Um ... yes, quite a few, actually," said Matthew, sounding a little more confident.

"Rather better than you've managed for the current piece," commented Simeon waspishly. "I think we should have a talk at some time about your marketing efforts."

"I'm sure some plays are easier to sell than others," said Ron in soothing tones, aiming to dispel the sudden tension which had arisen. "And 'Dream' has got to be one of Shakespeare's most popular pieces."

"Hmmm. Populist, I think perhaps you mean," replied Simeon dismissively. "Well, Matthew, have you arranged tickets for tonight's performance for our visitors here?"

Matthew look stricken. "No. I mean, I didn't know ..."

"Unfortunately, we haven't been able to take you up on your kind invitation," Tania intervened swiftly. "We had prior arrangements for tonight. Sorry."

"Well, that will be your loss," stated Simeon. "Although it's a pity. 'Anguish' is a deeply thoughtful piece of drama, but possibly wasted on the great mass of audiences. I dare say your people will be much more comfortable with your lightweight production of Shakespeare." It was impossible to ignore the sneering overtones in his words.

"And we're looking forward enormously to putting our lightweight production in front of *your* people to see how much they enjoy it," remarked Ron through slightly gritted teeth, his hackles obviously raised at Simeon's attitude.

"And we haven't got long to wait," Tania said hastily. "As my husband says, we're so looking forward to it. Anyway, we mustn't keep you, Simeon, must we, Ron? I'm sure you must have a million things to do." She favoured Matthew with a charming smile. "Goodbye."

"Yes, do come along, Matthew," snapped Simeon. "And for goodness sake, try to persuade that wretched dog of yours to keep up." He strode away, leaving Matthew to follow in his wake, an apologetic look on his face as he looked back over his shoulder.

"Well," said Ron, once the two were at a safe distance. "I don't think the reports of Mr Ashton-Rose have been exaggerated."

"He does seem to have a talent for unpleasantness," agreed Tania. "And that handshake of his! It was like fondling a slug! Yuk!"

Ron grimaced. "And on that delightful image, I think it's time we wended our way homewards. I for one could murder another cup of tea."

*

As the couple approached Hollyhock Cottage, they collided with a young woman in her late twenties who emerged at speed from the garden of one of the nearby houses. Soft brown curls formed a halo round a broad face which featured wide-awake grey eyes, partly concealed by large owlish spectacles, and a mouth, a touch too wide for perfection, which seemed apt to break into a smile at any moment.

"Oh, I'm so sorry," she apologised. "Are you all right? Only I wasn't looking where I was going."

"Not a problem," Ron reassured her. "Hardly any bones broken. I think I shall probably be all right for our performance of 'Swan Lake' next week."

"'Swan Lake'?" echoed the young woman, evidently baffled. "I didn't know anyone was doing ... I mean, it's not on my schedule or anything ..."

Tania laughed. "Pay no attention to him. He's just being over-dramatic as usual."

"Thank goodness for that," sighed the young woman in relief. "I thought for a horrible moment I'd got everything the wrong way round. Simeon would have slaughtered me."

"Of course, you work at the theatre, don't you?" enquired Tania.

"That's right. I do the sound and lighting."

"Then we shall be in your hands for the next week. I'm Tania Faye, and this is my husband Ron. We're in the Ramston production of 'Midsummer Night's Dream'. Which I'm fervently hoping does actually appear on your schedule."

"Nice to meet you properly. I'm Naomi Constantine. And don't worry. I've got the whole plot here in my folder." She gestured to the leather case under her arm. "Your director sent me very precise instructions as to what kind of music she wanted and when, so I've made sure everything is on disc as well as programmed into my computer."

"That sounds very organised," said Ron. "We shall look forward to hearing what you've got for us."

"Who are you playing?" enquired Naomi.

"Oh, just the usual doubling-up," replied Ron nonchalantly. "King and Queen of the Immortals, plus Theseus and Hippolyta."

"Oh, you're going to love what I've managed to sort out for your entrance in the forest in the hunting scene," enthused Naomi. "I've found a piece of Mahler which sounds so much like Mendelssohn that nobody could believe that it wasn't. Even Simeon, and he always knows exactly what's what."

"Bit of a taskmaster, is he?" asked Tania delicately.

"Well ..." Naomi seemed reluctant to be drawn. "He is the boss."

"Yes," said Ron. "You can tell."

"Of course, you've met him, haven't you?"

"You might say that," said Tania. "We had that rehearsal down at your Tithe Barn this morning, which he graced with his presence, together with your technical team, so I remember, with your responsibilities, you would have had to be there."

"I almost wasn't," replied Naomi. "I'd said I couldn't make it. I had an optician's appointment which I'd already had to put off twice, and these glasses are getting a bit past it. But I had to cancel it because Simeon wasn't best pleased."

"I can imagine," murmured Ron.

"And then we just ran into him a few minutes ago," continued Tania. "He was with ... Matthew, isn't it? They were out with their dog. We had a brief chat, but then Simeon seemed to be in some sort of a hurry, so off they went."

Naomi's hand went to her mouth. "Oh lord! That'll mean that he's probably got to the theatre already. I shall have to go. He always has a meeting for all the staff before the half-hour call to make sure everything is in order, and he'll murder me if I'm late again. I must go." She darted away.

"Well, I expect we shall see you tomorrow," called Tania after Naomi's rapidly retreating figure.

"Evidently another Simeon fan," remarked Ron wryly.

"Oh, he surely can't be all bad," said Tania. "Despite all the evidence to the contrary. He must have his good points, or else he wouldn't be in charge of one of the country's best-regarded theatres."

"Well, I think we've had quite enough of him for one day. Let's forget all about 'A Midsummer Night's Dream', the Mandyke Theatre, and its personnel and all their woes. I think we ought to take a leaf out of Leah's book, especially after all this unaccustomed fresh air and exercise this evening. So why don't we just go back to our cottage, put our feet up, and switch on the television? There must be something totally non-intellectual on to soothe our brains in anticipation of all the pate-cudgelling that's probably going to be happening next week. I seem to remember packing a rather nice bottle of Rioja in amongst our provisions, and I bet we can summon up enough appetite to put away a couple of the nibbles you've got in for the first night party, now that Toby's pitched in with his offer of hospitality."

"That suits me," smiled Tania, linking her arm with her husband's, as the couple resumed their stroll in the direction of Hollyhock Cottage.

Chapter 7
Sunday

"Time's getting on," called Ron. "It's almost quarter to ten. And we don't want to be the last there."

"I'm just finishing doing some sandwiches," floated Tania's voice from the kitchen. "We're bound to need something along the way to keep the wolf from the door. And you know what get-in day is like," she continued, appearing in the doorway to the sitting room. "Totally unpredictable, and probably even more so in a theatre none of us has ever worked at before."

"Well, at least that stage manager chap seems very efficient," remarked Ron. "I get the impression he runs a pretty tight ship. Plus he must be used to shepherding first-timers around the place. I'm not worried."

"Tell me that again in six hours when nothing is in the right place, nobody's had a chance to deliver a line, and Leah is tearing her hair out and about to strangle the nearest person," retorted Tania with a smile. "Anyway, I'm ready to roll. I'll just put the provisions in my bag. Have you got our make-up kits?"

"All cleaned, checked, and standing by," said Ron, pointing to two matching plastic toolboxes waiting on the table by the front door.

"Then let's go." Tania disappeared into the kitchen, returning immediately carrying a capacious shoulder-bag, and the two made their way out into a bright sunlit Fore Street.

*

The group of performers gathered outside the front of the White House were chatting amongst themselves with an air of mild excitement as Tania and Ron approached, and Hamlet broke away from them to greet the couple with an exuberant fusillade of barking.

"Good grief," said Peter Talbot, as he retrieved his

joyously cavorting pet. "We've managed not to be the last to arrive. That must be some sort of record." He looked around the group. "So ... '*Is all our company here?*', as one might say."

"Oi, you!" His wife nudged him playfully in the ribs. "Get off my lines!"

"And actually, 'no' would seem to be the answer," chuckled Peter, unrepentant. "We're missing Leah."

At that moment, with a fearsome grinding of gears, a white van which had clearly seen better days made its way round the corner of the lane and up to where the group was waiting, and Leah clambered down from the driving seat. "Sorry if I've kept you all waiting," she declared, with a look of disdain towards her vehicle. "But this ghastly old crate refused to start first time. Or even seventh. However ..." She let out a gusty sigh. "... I'm here..." She looked at her watch. "... and not actually late, so I've managed to avoid giving you lot any hostages to fortune." She uttered her characteristic bark of laughter. "So, I'm assuming somebody will appear and let us know what's on the schedule."

As she spoke, the front door of the White House opened, and Luke Crowan emerged. "Good morning, everyone. My name is Luke, and I'm in charge of front-of-house for the Mandyke Theatre. And I'm sure I speak for everyone when I say that we're delighted to welcome your production and its performers. In fact, I've met a couple of you already ..." He gave a friendly nod in the direction of Tania and Ron, who smiled back. "... and our whole team will be glad to get to know you and help you in whatever way we can. Now our stage manager Reuben and his team, some of whom I think have already been introduced to you, are already down on the stage, but I'd like to start with a sort of orientation tour of things up here before I hand you over to them."

Leah stepped forward. "Pleased to meet you, Luke.

I'm Leah Sutherland." The two shook hands. "And I, for my sins, am the director of this untalented mob, and I'll try to keep them under some sort of control this week." A good-humoured smile accompanied her words.

"I see we shall all get on famously," grinned Luke in response. "So, if everyone would like to follow me." He led the way through the front door, with the company at his heels.

The entrance hall of the White House was a masterpiece of Art Deco design. Oval in shape, the white walls were subtly embellished with panelled motifs in the palest mint green, with a delicately-moulded cornice above which rose a shallow dome illuminated by concealed lighting. Doors in pale wood with angular inlays of parquetry were symmetrically situated around the room. A wrought-iron-banistered staircase rose at the rear.

"Oh, this is marvellous," declared Leah. "And I swear, the next time I do a Noël Coward, this is going to be my set design."

"Glad you like it," said Luke. "We're very proud of the fact that the trustees of the theatre have always tried to keep as much of the house intact as possible. Of course, there have been a few changes. Now through here ..." He opened one of the doors. "... we have what used to be the dining room, which led into the sitting room overlooking the sea. We use the two rooms as the cafe and bar during performances. And over there is what used to be a study, which is now my office, although I'm afraid my computer tends to diminish the 1930s authenticity somewhat. And that door there used to be the kitchen – well, it still is, in a way, except that the original has been carved up to make a small kitchen to provide for the cafe, and the other absolute essential for the audience in a place like this ... plenty of loos!"

"Pleased to hear it," remarked Martha Talbot. "If

there's one thing I hate, it's having to hang about in the wings, waiting to take up the second act because there's still a queue for the Ladies."

"We aim to please," smiled Luke. "So, if you'd all like to come this way, we'll head on out to the terrace." He made his way through the bar and out through a set of French windows, emerging at the rear of the house, and then stood back and waited for a reaction. He was not disappointed. There was a chorus of 'Wow', 'That is some view', and 'This is fabulous', topped off with a youthful cry of 'Look, mummy, there's a whale!'.

"I think it's a dolphin, Zak darling," murmured Elizabeth, "but it's still very exciting. And see, down there is the stage where we're all going to be doing our play. Won't that be fun?"

"And whose," came a sudden thundering interruption from above the company's heads, breaking the mood of happy delight, "is that pile of scrap metal outside the front of my house?"

Everyone looked up, to see an irate Simeon Ashton-Rose, clad in a peacock-blue dressing-gown, leaning over the balustrade of a balcony on the first floor.

Leah stepped forward. "I assume, Mr Ashton-Rose, you are referring to my vehicle," she said icily. "Which contains the costumes and props for our production. And in which I have just arrived. Am I to deduce that you are not happy with its location?"

"Not the most difficult deduction you'll ever make," snapped Simeon. "And I should be grateful if you would remove it. Immediately."

"Leave it with me, Simeon," called Luke in emollient tones. "I'll show the lady the way down to the unloading area."

"Do that." With a whirl of brightly-coloured silk, Simeon turned and disappeared.

"Sorry about that," apologised Luke to Leah. "I

wasn't expecting a visitation from His Majesty just yet. And I'm told he's never at his best first thing in the morning."

"First thing?" muttered Leah, eyebrows raised as she glanced at her watch. "Not exactly what I'd call it, but heigh-ho. I hadn't realised that your Mr Ashton-Rose lived over the shop, so to speak."

"Oh yes. He and Matt have got the whole of the top floor of the house as an apartment. Very stylish, I gather, although I've never been invited."

"He and Matt?" echoed Leah.

"That's right," replied Luke. And in reply to Leah's look of enquiry, "Matthew Sutcombe, the one who runs our box office. They're an item. Have been for a while now, ever since Matt came down to do a summer job helping backstage with one of the touring pro productions and sort of never left."

"Ah yes. The young man who was at his elbow when he came to our rehearsal meeting. Well, no accounting for taste on his part," said Leah, rolling her eyes slightly. "However ..." She turned to the rest of the company, who had been listening with interest to the entire incident, "Everybody, why don't you all go on down to the stage while I move my van." She scanned the group. "And Paul, Timothy, James and Thomas – if you can find your way around to where I'm parked, you can help with the unloading. Right, Luke. Which way do I go?" The two disappeared back into the house.

"Watch your step," Ron warned Tania, as everyone cautiously made their way down the steeply-raked centre aisle of the auditorium, to where a group of people, led by Reuben Hawke, were just emerging at one side of the stage.

"Good morning, all," Reuben greeted them as they arrived at the playing level at the bottom. "I hope you've all had a good night's sleep and are raring to go with setting up for your production. I know we're all looking forward to helping you. And I know that some of you have already met some of us, but let me refresh your memories by introducing the team. I'm Reuben, your stage manager, and this here is Ruth Tresillian, who is my trusty assistant S.M." He gestured to the young woman at his side. "Mary Pengelly over there will be helping you with your props – that's when she's not rushing about serving up in the cafe and bar – very good at multi-tasking, is our Mary – so she'll show you where the props room is." Mary gave a cheery smile and a wave to Tania and Ron. "And that young lady at the back is Naomi Constantine, and she is our wizard in charge of lighting and sound." Naomi, from the rear of the group, gave a little wave. "And that is us. And I expect we shall all get to know each other very quickly." Reuben looked around. "But I don't see your director. Is she not with you?"

"She's just moving her vehicle with all our bits and pieces in it," volunteered David. "Your artistic director chap wasn't best pleased with its being parked out front."

"Oh, you've already managed a little run-in with Simeon, have you?" smiled Reuben. "Oh well, start as you mean to go on," he murmured to himself.

At that moment, a rattling and jolting sound, accompanied by a resounding backfire, announced the arrival of Leah's van just off the side of the stage. "Come along, you lads," she demanded, appearing in an archway. "Let's get everything through as quick as you can, and then we'll sort out where it all goes. Oh, hello, Reuben. Back in a jiff." She disappeared back outside, while all her Ramston colleagues followed in an effort to help, and soon everything was piled in a heap in the middle of the stage area.

"Two questions," said Reuben as he surveyed the stack of items. "What furniture and scenery are you using

76

where, and do they stay in position the whole time?"

"We've kept it to a minimum," replied Leah. "There's the mossy bank, which goes roughly in the centre of stage left. In fact, I thought that the low raised area indicated on the stage plan I was sent looked ideal." She cast an eye over that part of the acting area. "Which it looks to be. But it does have to go, once the lovers have been discovered in the forest, to give space for the Mechanicals' play. The only thing is, where do we put it?"

"That's not a problem," answered Reuben. "There's space for it behind the wall to the right of that arch." He pointed. "But you do know that we don't provide stagehands to move scenery, don't you?"

"I'm ahead of you. Once Bottom has woken up, the two chaps playing Demetrius and Lysander are free to nip in and move the bank during the scene in Quince's house. That's the way we've done it at rehearsal."

"You do realise how heavy that thing is, don't you, Leah?" spoke up Paul.

"Then you'd both better make sure you have your porridge for breakfast, hadn't you, gentlemen?" retorted Leah.

"Anything else?" asked Reuben.

"Only the two thrones for Theseus and Hippolyta in the play scene. Which I've placed centre right, again on the raised portion."

"Then that's easy. We can keep them just offstage on that side, and they can be placed in position at the appropriate moment. Perhaps at the end of the Quince's house scene?"

"You do know the play," smiled Leah admiringly. "And that's ideal, because when Flute and Snug go off then, they can put the thrones in place before they go to change. Got that, James and Thomas?"

"Okay, Leah!" chorused the cousins.

"And that's it as far as the major items go. Now we

just have the costumes and props to sort out. And nobody's yet mentioned dressing rooms." Leah looked around. "Please don't tell me that the cast have to go all the way up to the house."

Reuben gave a chuckle of amusement. "Fortunately, no. Allow me to let you into the secret of the Mandyke Theatre." He gestured to what appeared to be an alcove in the rocks adjacent to the way through to the place where the van was parked. "So if I can enlist the help of your young gentlemen to put your scenery items into position ..." He looked across to where his young assistant was hovering on the fringe of the group. "Ruth, perhaps you'd like to show Ms. Sutherland the way."

"Come on, Ron," whispered Tania to her husband. "Let's see what this mysterious secret is." The couple followed on, as Ruth led Leah into the alcove.

"Oh, this is amazing." Leah stood astonished, as what appeared to be nothing but a recess suddenly opened up into a passageway cut into the rock, lit with fluorescent lighting, which looked as if it carried around in a semicircle under the lowest rows of auditorium seating. "How on earth ..." She stood, lost for words.

"It's the only way to get from one side of the stage to the other," explained Ruth in her soft voice.

"Because, of course, you can't rush round backstage as you would in an ordinary theatre," nodded Leah.

"No," said Ruth. "You'd end up at the bottom of the cliff if you tried." She gave a small shy smile.

"But how ... I mean, who ... this must have taken forever." Leah was still taken aback.

"Reuben says that it was all done in the old ladies' time. I don't really know. I've only been involved with the theatre for a year, since I came down from uni. But according to Reuben, there were a lot of tin mines closing down in the area at the time the old ladies were starting the theatre, and they gave work to some of the miners who would have been unemployed and starving otherwise. At least, that's the story. So the miners cut this corridor ..." Ruth moved further onward. "... and they also cut out rooms under the cliff which we use as dressing rooms and props store." She indicated doors at intervals along the passageway.

"And what's up here?" enquired Ron from the rear of the group. To their left, a rock-cut staircase vanished upwards into darkness.

"That leads to the sound and lighting box," said Ruth. "It's just above our heads. It's another room, and there's a sort of letterbox opening hidden among the audience seating so that Naomi can see the stage."

"This is quite something," breathed Tania to Ron. "But I hope none of our people suffer from claustrophobia. Well, I suppose we shall soon find out." The pair followed in the footsteps of Ruth and Leah, emerging at the opposite corner of the stage area from their point of entry, to find the members of the cast standing on the stage as if waiting for instructions.

Leah clapped her hands to gain their attention. "Right, everybody. Let's get these hampers of costumes and props sorted out, and then we can allocate your dressing rooms and make a start on the technicalities. Paul! Timothy! Thomas and James! Don't all just stand there as if tomorrow will do. Let's make use of those youthful muscles of yours. You can start bringing the hampers through, and perhaps the ladies can assist you in sorting out the costumes and allocating dressing rooms."

"Shall I show them where to go?" volunteered Ruth.

"That would be very kind," said Leah. "Now, props."

"Would you like me to show you where the props room is?" asked Mary, stepping forward.

"Excellent idea. Not that we have all that many. You

other chaps, can you gather up the other boxes and the cushions and take them to where this lady will show you? And I think my time would be best spent going with Naomi here, and starting to go through the sound and light plot in her secret lair, which I'm told is hidden somewhere in the cliff."

"Oh, you've heard about the old smugglers' tunnel, have you?" enquired Reuben with a smile.

Leah looked puzzled. "I beg your pardon?"

Reuben laughed. "It's nothing of the sort really. It's just a local tale. Apparently, when the old tin miners were excavating out the passage and the rooms in the cliff, they came across a bit of a shaft. Probably some sort of abandoned working for a tin mine that never got dug, but somebody got hold of the story and decided that it was a secret passage for smugglers between the cove and the cellars of the old cottage that used to be where the White House is. All nonsense, of course, but people love a tale. But now that it's widened out with proper steps and lights, we use it for getting actors up to the top of the theatre without needing to go round the sides in full sight."

"Fascinating," remarked Leah. "But no time for romancing. Right, everyone – to work!"

Chapter 8
Sunday

"How do you want to tackle this, Ms Sutherland?" asked Reuben Hawke, as the last of the items of scenery, the substantial 'mossy bank', was placed in its off-stage position with a resounding thump and a cry from Timothy of 'Mind my toes!'.

"Just Leah, please," replied the director absently, her mind clearly occupied with a plethora of thoughts. After a few moments pause, during which the remaining members of the theatre's stage crew gathered themselves behind Reuben, while the play's cast formed a loose group in the centre of the stage, she came back into focus and took a look at her watch. "Okay, everybody," she announced. "Here's the plan. First off, we'll do a top-and-tail technical rehearsal of the whole play. And that, for the benefit of our younger members," she added, looking at the Kent children who were gazing up at her, somewhat in awe, "means that we will begin at the beginning and do the start and finish of each scene, including any sound and light cues and costume changes, but without all the speeches in between. Everybody clear?" Nods all round. "Now, I assume you've organised the dressing rooms?"

"All done," said Elizabeth Kent. "Ruth helped me sort things out, and she's made sure we've all got enough costume rails. Ron and Tania are in 'A', and Peter and Andrew are next door in 'B'. With Hamlet," she added.

"I hope that place is soundproofed," growled Leah. "The last thing we need is for that blasted dog to take it into his head to start barking over something stupid at a crucial moment."

"You needn't worry," Reuben reassured her. "Because everything is all cut into the rock, you can't hear a thing, either in or coming from the dressing rooms. That's why we've got a speaker in each one so that the cast know where we are in the performance without needing to come rubber-necking in the wings."

"Glad to hear it."

"Maybe somebody ought to go into the butcher's shop up in the village and see if they can supply some bones," suggested Tania. "That'll help keep Hamlet quiet."

"I could do that," said Ruth. "It's my uncle's shop. I'm sure he wouldn't mind. He always lets me have bones for Matthew's dog."

"Good," said Leah drily. "Well, that's one cast member catered for. And what about the others, Elizabeth? Just in case I need to track somebody down. Not that I'm likely to, you understand. You all know my rule. No directors backstage during the performance."

"Martha and the girls are in 'C'," continued Elizabeth. "That's the lot on stage right. And then the props room is half-way along the corridor, and after that it's dressing room 'D', which has got the four boys in it ..."

"And there's a recipe for trouble," murmured Leah under her breath.

"... and David and I and the children are in 'E' at the stage left end."

"Props? All sorted?"

"Everything's laid out on tables in the props room," explained Mary Pengelly. "I've done what we usually do. I've checked with everyone who handles a prop, although you haven't got that many with this play, and of course I can't be around to help because I shall be busy up at the house helping with the catering. But we've taped an outline of all the various bits and pieces on the tables, like we always do, so that you know if anything's not there because you can see where everything goes."

"Like they do with the tape around a dead body in a crime movie?" laughed Paul. "'The Case of the Missing

Manuscript'. 'Who stole my scroll?'."

"You'd be the first to complain if one of your props wasn't there when you needed it," said Leah. "So be grateful, young man."

"But I'm going to be there most of the time anyway," said Ruth quickly. "So I can keep an eye on things, and help if I'm needed."

"Good," nodded Leah. "That sounds very organised. And lastly, Reuben, how about the FX?"

"As far as I know, Naomi has everything under control as regards effects, both light and sound," he replied. "If you want to sit up in her control box with her during the run-through, you can tweak any sound cues that need to be modified." He glanced up at the clear blue sky. "And as for light cues, I don't think it'll be worth bothering with those today, do you?"

"Probably not," agreed Leah with a laugh. "And there aren't that many anyway. But at least we can make sure they're marked for the evening rehearsals."

"And you may not need too much in the way of extra lighting, even then," pointed out Naomi. "Sometimes when the sky is clear and it's a full moon, like it will be this week, it can get so bright out here you can read a newspaper. I might be out of a job!" she smiled.

"Surely not," smiled Leah in response. "So, if there's nothing else, why don't you and I go up to your box and you can play me the music you've recorded while everybody else gets ready. And Reuben, if you can call 'Beginners' in fifteen minutes, please. Let's go."

In a sudden burst of activity, the company dispersed.

*

"So," said Leah, closing her notebook and letting out a deep sigh. "That's all my notes for you. Does anyone have any questions for me?" A forest of hands shot up, and she let out her customary bark of laughter. "And that will teach me! As that ex-husband of mine once told me, never ask a question you don't already know the answer to. But that's the start of a very long tale, and one that we won't be going into today!" She cast her eye around the group. "Ron, you first. Problem?"

"Not really, Leah," replied Ron. "And I know we've only been topping and tailing, but I'm slightly worried that I may not have time to make my costume changes from one character to the other. Because for some of them, I have to get right across to the opposite side of the stage from my exit. I mean, you don't want Duke Theseus coming on half-dressed as King of the Fairies, do you?"

Leah suppressed a smile. "I think that will be the least of our worries, what with all the confusions between the lovers and Puck's other shenanigans. But you did all the changes this time, didn't you?"

"Just. It was a pretty close-run thing a couple of times," admitted Ron.

"And you will get quicker as we go on," Leah reassured him. "But if you're that concerned, why don't you have someone standing by to help you?"

"I can do that, Leah," volunteered Peter. "After all, Egeus isn't on that much, and I'm in the next-door dressing room."

"Well then, problem solved. Next?"

"I've got something," spoke up James. "It's my lion costume."

"Which I thought was extremely impressive," responded Leah with a touch of severity. "I hope I'm not going to have to tell our wardrobe ladies that you've been complaining."

"Oh no, not really," James hastily back-pedalled. "It's just that whenever I take a deep breath to roar, I get a mouth full of bits of string from the mane. I think it needs a bit of a haircut."

"Fashionable short-back-and-sides?" queried Leah, one eyebrow raised. "Not exactly the look we were aiming for. And to think that, a few years back, I could have cast any one of a number of young men with curls down to their shoulders. What's the modern theatre come to, I wonder?" she declaimed, an unexpected twinkle in her eye betraying the fact that the complaint was not to be taken too seriously.

Esther raised a hand. "I could take a look at it and give it a gentle trim if you like. That's if you trust me, Leah."

"Do you know, I rather think I do. I knew there was a reason for casting a hairdresser as Hermia. Apart from your brilliant audition, of course, my dear. So yes, I'm happy to leave that with you. But don't go too mad. I want a lion, not a shorn sheep. Who's next? Martha?"

"It's Quince's quill." Martha held up a very sorry-looking feather, drooping alarmingly from a bend in the shaft. "I had that bit of business with the script with Bottom, and we collided and broke my pen. I can't go on with it like this."

"Can't you just tape it up?" proposed Andrew. "And maybe try not to bash into me next time?" He was rewarded with a glare.

"There's loads of seagulls around here," suggested Thomas. "Why don't James and I go down to the harbour and try to catch one and pinch a feather?"

"Not a good idea," said Leah. "The last thing I want is a rerun of 'The Birds', with you being pursued by enraged seagulls."

"Don't worry, Leah," said Mary. "I've just thought. I might have just the thing up in the props store in the barn. There's a large bronze feather from when we did one of the Roman plays, and I'm sure it would do the trick. I think it's in the 'Titus Andronicus' box. I'll sort it out when I go up later."

"Excellent." Leah thought for a moment. "Anything else? No?" She looked at her watch. "Two o'clock. In that case, I have some very good news for you. I was very pleased with the way that run-through went, so as far as technical matters go, I think we're ready for dress rehearsal. And after our script run-through yesterday, I can say pretty much the same thing as regards the performance. So, not wishing to over-egg the pudding, I'm going to give you all the rest of the day off." A muted cheer and a ripple of applause arose from the cast. "So go and have your Sunday lunch or whatever, even though it's a little past lunchtime, and enjoy the remainder of your day of rest. Then tomorrow, I won't be calling you during the day, but don't take that as an excuse not to take a look at your scripts and make sure that anything that wasn't perfect today gets looked at. And then, if Reuben is in agreement ..." A sideways look at the stage manager. "... we'll go for a full rehearsal at seven-thirty tomorrow evening."

"Fine by us, Leah," said Reuben, with accompanying nods from his colleagues.

"Thank you then, everyone. Go and get changed. That's it for today."

*

A cacophony of ferociously grinding gears heralded the departure of Leah's van, as the cast of the play emerged on to the stage area and began to make their way up through the auditorium towards the exit at the side of the White House. As Ron and Tania were about to follow in their footsteps, Tania stopped abruptly and, with a muttered 'Oh blast!', suddenly turned and rushed back in the direction of the entrance to the dressing room corridor, almost colliding with Mary Pengelly as she emerged.

"What's all that about?" queried Mary. "Is there a problem?"

"I doubt it," laughed Ron in response. "She's probably just forgotten something."

His words were proved correct as, a few moments later, Tania reappeared waving her phone in triumph. "Got it," she cried. "I'd put one of my headdresses on top of it on the dressing table."

"You are forever leaving that thing about the house and then having to go hunting for it," smiled Ron indulgently. "How many times have I said, put it in one place and then you'll know where it is."

"Still, you've got it, so no harm done," said Mary. "Talking of which, how were the props? Did my little system work for you?"

"Perfectly," replied Ron, as the three began to climb the steep steps up towards the back of the theatre seating. "Not that I put your system to too severe a test. My magic flower was easy to spot, and that's the only prop I have anything to do with. And I didn't hear any complaints from any of the others, so I assume they were all just as happy."

"So just Quince's quill to sort out," remarked Tania.

Mary's hand went to her mouth. "Oh lord! I'd almost forgotten that. Thank you for the reminder, my love. I'll go and dig that out now. I've just got time before I have to take over from my sister at the cafe."

"You're open today?" queried Ron.

"Course we are. Sunday's one of our best days."

"I'm surprised you can be spared today, in that case," remarked Tania.

"Oh, it's always like this when we've got a new play coming in," said Mary. "But all Judith's girls are quite capable of running the place until I get there, so there's no worry. But I'd better scoot off," she added, as the three emerged through the side gate on to the lane in front of the White House. "I'll see you later." With a cheery wave, she was gone.

"What's the plan now, love?" asked Ron. "That's if we have one."

"I don't really know," said Tania. "I didn't expect us to have been let off this early, so I've got our picnic lunch in my bag."

"Then let's take advantage." Ron pondered for a moment. "Here's a thought. Why don't we take that road down to the harbour and have our lunch there? From what little I've glimpsed, it looks rather charming, and there's bound to be somewhere we can sit and have a picnic. That's if we can fend off any marauding seagulls," he added with a smile. "You know what a reputation they have. And then maybe we can go back to the Pilchard's Arms again for dinner this evening."

"I like it. Let's go. But on one condition," added Tania, as the couple began to descend the lane alongside St. Petroc's church. "Before I break out the provisions, I shall make sure I put on plenty of the sunscreen which I did actually remember to put in the bag, in spite of certain persons who accuse me of forgetfulness. I was afraid that we might get too much sun if we spent a lot of time out on stage in this weather. And the last thing you need," she remarked with a smile, "is a Queen of the Amazons with a red peeling nose. Not an attractive look."

"Your nose will always be attractive," laughed Ron, depositing a kiss on the tip. "Now," he said, looking around as the pair reached the harbour, "where's a good spot to sit?"

Despite the many tourists who were dotted around the area, mostly family groups consisting of ambling inattentive fathers, harassed mothers, and children displaying an alarming tendency to rush off in unexpected directions or else to smear themselves with the residue of dripping ice cream cornets, the couple found a tree-shaded bench alongside a quiet corner of the harbour. Sandwiches consumed with a minimum of interference from the local wildlife, and washed down with a couple of cans of shandy which Tania unexpectedly produced from the depths of her backpack, the pair decided to indulge in a little gentle exploration. The harbour wall, constructed from massive rough chunks of granite which looked to have been withstanding the assault of Atlantic breakers for centuries, formed a picturesque walk, giving a different view of the sheltered basin with its mixture of colourful pleasure craft of all sizes and the more workaday local fishing boats, many festooned with trawl nets drying in the sun. A tiny ancient warehouse huddled in the lee of the highest part of the wall proudly proclaimed itself to be 'Cornwall's Only Authentic Smugglers' Museum'. And alongside the landward side of the harbour, a row of erstwhile fishermen's cottages, some bearing their original tarred protection while others had been painted in a variety of pastel colours, had been turned into business premises. 'The Harbour Gallery' displayed a selection of watercolours of local scenes, together with an artistic display of carved wooden sea creatures amidst coloured glass fishing floats and lobster pots. 'Nipper's Nook' advertised 'The County's Finest Crab Sandwiches', in amongst its extensive menu of all kinds of seafood. 'Madame Demelza', behind her beaded curtain, promised insights into the future. And next door 'The Rockery', behind rather dusty bottle-glass windows, offered a muddled mingling of fossils and carved stone items which proved irresistible to Tania.

"Oh Ron, we have to look in here," she declared, and without waiting for a response, ducked her head to pass through the shop's low doorway and stepped down on to the flag-stoned floor. The dimly-lit interior was full of glass-fronted display cases packed with items of jewellery, while rickety tables held teetering piles of Chinese plates, carved wooden boxes, pieces of driftwood in convoluted baroque shapes, and porcelain hands whose fingers sported rings ranging from the exquisite to the bizarre. Plaster gargoyles glared down from the walls, while trilobites threatened to scuttle out from dark corners. Geodes in jewel colours sparkled under spotlights in corner cabinets, while on the floor their massive purple amethyst cousins presented trip hazards for the unwary. And one display drew Tania's particular attention. "Ron, look at these," she breathed.

The case held a bewildering menagerie of animals, all carved from semi-precious stones. There were malachite tigers cheek by jowl with labradorite wolves. A family of jade pandas shared a shelf with a shoal of quartz crystal fish and a group of rhodochrosite penguins. A soapstone bull stood alongside a haematite rabbit and a jasper squirrel, while a rose quartz pig peered out from between a pair of amber dogs, as a crocodile in lapis lazuli looked on. Tiny onyx dinosaurs huddled together as if fearing extinction. But the creature which caught Tania's eye nestled half-hidden behind a chalcedony eagle.

"Ron, I adore that little bear," she said. The animal, only two inches long, was carved from a watery green fluorite with hints of pink, its eyes picked out as two tiny black dots in a face which, for all its simplicity, seemed to wear an encouragingly friendly expression. "He's just delightful. And isn't fluorite supposed to have healing properties?"

"The young lady's not wrong," came an unexpected voice from behind the couple. They turned, to see a tiny wizened elderly woman in a concealed doorway in the wall between the shop and the adjoining building, who must have entered unobserved since they arrived. "Fluorite is a protector," she continued in a deep Cornish burr. "And it attunes with the soul. The more you handle it, the more it becomes as one with you."

"Umm ... that's ... er ... fascinating," said Ron, uncertain how to react. "I was just wondering how much it was."

"Would you like to hold him, my dear?" enquired the woman, ignoring Ron.

"Well, if I may," said Tania. The woman shuffled forward, opened the case, reached in for the bear, and placed it on Tania's outstretched palm. "Oh, I love him," she murmured after a few moments. She looked at her husband. "Ron, please ...?"

Ron smiled. "Oh, all right. So, what do we owe you, ma'am?"

The woman took a long look at the bear, before reaching out and closing Tania's fingers over it. "Keep him, my dear. He's yours. I can see he likes you."

"Oh, I couldn't possibly," protested Tania. "We must pay you."

"Just keep him safe, and he'll keep you safe," responded the woman. "Everyone needs protection at one time or another. But remember to keep him out of the sun. The sun will weaken him. But moonlight will be his friend. And yours."

"Well, if you're sure ..." Tania opened her hand. "Ron, he is beautiful, isn't he?" The couple pored over the tiny animal, before she continued, "And we'll take great care of him, I promise." She looked up, intending to thank the woman once again, but she had disappeared as silently as she arrived.

Chapter 9
Sunday

"Well, that was unexpected," remarked Ron, as the couple headed for the lane to take them back up towards the village. "Odd. And generous. I wonder why."

"Perhaps it just proves that there are still some good people about," replied Tania, smiling down fondly at the little bear figure still clutched in her hand.

"But it seemed all very mystic," persisted Ron. A thought struck him. "Do you suppose that was Madame Demelza herself?"

Tania considered. "Do you know, I think you must be right. The shop was right next to her place, and she did seem to appear through the wall."

"And how many strange old dames with odd powers are there in the average West Country village, I wonder?"

"More than you'd think, I dare say," laughed Tania. "After all, this is Cornwall. Actually, she put me in mind of nothing so much as a sort of reincarnation of Dolly Pentreath."

"Who?"

"The last person to speak Cornish as her native language," explained Tania. "Seventeen-hundred-and-something, I think. I remember reading about her somewhere."

"Reincarnation?" chuckled Ron. "That old woman looked to me as if she might well have dated from the seventeen hundreds. All she needed was a black cat, and I could quite easily believe in supernatural powers being at work in Polkernow."

"Well, obviously!" retorted Tania. "Because otherwise you would be about to give a very unconvincing portrayal as King of the supernatural inhabitants of Fairyland!"

"Touché," said Ron. "I shall make sure I channel Madame Demelza as soon as I step on stage. But for the moment," he added, puffing slightly, "I'm concentrating on getting up this hill. It didn't seem this steep on the way down. I am going to need my siesta."

*

Ron stretched lazily as he surfaced gradually from a deep sleep. For a moment he blinked, puzzled, at the unfamiliar ceiling above him, before his brain came slowly into focus. He turned his head, and his gaze fell upon the figure of the woman lying alongside him, her deep breathing speckled with an occasional tiny snuffle. He smiled fondly, and rolled over carefully in order to reach the watch on the cabinet next to the bed, and his eyes widened with surprise as he realised the time. Rolling back, he propped himself up on one elbow before leaning forward to deposit a gentle kiss on his companion's brow. The eyes in front of him opened slowly.

"Good afternoon, Mrs Faye," he murmured. "Although," he added with a twinkle, "it's probably more accurate to say 'good evening'."

Tania's eyes jerked wide open, and she sat up abruptly. "What?"

Ron chuckled. "Calm down, love. No panic. It's not as if we've got places to go and people to see. I'm just saying that the time seems to have disappeared while we were having our little snooze."

Tania gave a long deep sigh as she lay back down alongside her husband. "Sorry – for a second, I couldn't think where I was, or when. I must have gone out like a light."

"I think we both did," agreed Ron.

"Must have been all that fresh air and exercise from earlier."

"Right," said Ron. "All that unaccustomed fresh sea

air and vigorous exercise," he echoed. "Although," he added with a roguish grin, "some of our most recent exercise wasn't all that unaccustomed, if I remember rightly."

Tania gave a pretty blush. "You, Mr Faye, are a wicked man," she said, giving him a playful slap. "All I wanted was a little nap. I blame you entirely."

"Guilty as charged." Ron stretched again, a contented smile on his face. "But I suppose we ought to make a move."

"Why? What time is it?"

Ron reached out to take another look at his watch. "Let's put it this way, love. I think we're probably a bit too late for one of Judith Polkerris's cream teas. But on the other hand, I think I may well have worked up enough appetite for a bite of dinner at the Pilchard's Arms." He swung round to place his feet on the floor. "So I intend to grab a shower and a shave in order to make myself fit to be seen in public with my lovely wife. That is, unless you want the bathroom first."

"No, you go ahead," replied Tania, sinking back into the pillows. "I'm just going to have another five minutes."

"Unaccustomed exercise," sang Ron under his breath, just managing to escape into the bathroom as the cushion thrown after him by Tania hit the closing door.

*

Fore Street lay bathed in evening sunlight as the couple strolled down towards the pub, and as they entered the bar of the Pilchard's Arms they were surprised at the lack of customers. A pair of elderly men, obviously locals, were engrossed in a lively game of cribbage in one corner, while one of the dining booths was occupied by a young man and woman, apparently scarcely out of their teens, who seemed deeply engrossed in each other. Apart from that, the place was empty.

"You seem very quiet this evening, Toby,"

remarked Ron, as the landlord stepped forward to greet the new arrivals.

"Nothing unusual for a Sunday night," replied Toby comfortably. "You should have seen it in here this lunchtime. Run off our feet, we were. But the evening's a different thing. All the day tourists have gone home, see, and a lot of the folks from up away at the caravan park are busy packing before they set off up country in the morning. So we get a chance to catch our breath a bit."

"I hope we're not too late for something to eat?" wondered Tania. "You haven't closed down the kitchen, have you?"

"Ah no," chuckled Toby. "We're a bit like the old Windmill Theatre. We never close – well, not for good friends, anyway, which is what I'm thinking you Ramston people are."

Tania was surprised at the accolade. "That's very nice of you."

"Some of the theatre groups we get coming down here get a bit high and mighty," confided Toby. "Too big for their boots. Think a lot of themselves. Rather like ..." He stopped abruptly.

"Like ...?" queried Ron in an encouraging tone. "Or can I guess? Your friendly local theatre artistic director, perhaps?"

"Not that friendly, Ron," his wife corrected him. "Unless you've forgotten that little episode this morning."

"Simeon been kicking off again?" said Toby. "Not that I'd be surprised. That man has a talent for making trouble." He took a breath. "Anyway, let's not spoil your evening talking about him. I'd much rather spend my time thinking about pleasant people. Like that bunch of your youngsters I've got staying here."

"Paul and Timothy and the girls, do you mean?"

"That's right. Now I know some people do go on a lot about the youth of today and how as they've got no manners and whatnot, but they came and had some supper here earlier on and they were as nice as pie. Made a point of complimenting my Angela on her food, and they insisted on buying her a drink before they went off."

"Went off?" queried Ron.

"That's right. They've gone into Penzance looking for a bit of nightlife. Can't say as I blame them – Polkernow isn't exactly Ibiza when it comes to clubbing, is it?" Toby laughed. "The Mumming's about as lively as we get round here. As you will see on Wednesday. Not forgetting the Feast on Tuesday, of course. Speaking of which, here's me going on and on, and you want something to eat this evening."

"Any suggestions?" asked Tania.

"Well," said Toby, considering, "if you're up for a bit of stew, we've got one of Angela's specialities on the hob. All local too. It's shin of beef from Tresillian's, casseroled with red onions from Godolphin's Farm up the valley, together with a special dark ale from the old brewery in Truro. Melts in the mouth, it does. Taters from Godolphin's as well. How does that sound?"

"Wonderful," enthused Ron, after exchanging glances with his wife.

"And a pint of Badger's Butt to go with it? I think that always goes down well with a stew. And a G & T for the lady?"

"We are in your hands," smiled Tania happily, and the couple turned to take their seats in one of the booths.

*

"I can tell you didn't enjoy that," remarked Toby, as he came to collect the empty plates some time later. "My old mum used to say, 'A clean plate's the best compliment a cook can get'."

"She wasn't wrong," replied Ron, sighing contentedly. "That was absolutely delicious."

"So, how about afters?"

"I couldn't eat another thing," protested Tania. "We aren't really great meat-eaters, and that stew was very filling."

"Ah, well, that's quality, you see. Bodmin Moor beef, that was. Abel Tresillian, he always makes sure we get the finest meat he can lay his hands on. He's got a deal with one of the farmers up there to supply all the stuff for his shop."

"Of course, he's your local butcher across the road, isn't he? We met his niece Ruth. She's part of the backstage team for our play, and she said she could get hold of some bones for us."

"Bones?" Toby sounded puzzled.

"We have a rather large dog in the cast," explained Tania, laughing. "Hamlet. He's more of a stage prop really, just to make things look good when Ron and I turn up hunting in one of the forest scenes, but we had to include him because otherwise his owners wouldn't have been able to be in the play. They'd never come away leaving him in a kennel, because he's a bit of a handful. So Ruth said she'd get hold of some bones to help keep him occupied. She seems lovely."

"I see," said Toby. His brow creased. "Poor Ruth. Oh well ..."

Tania's ear's pricked up. "Why 'poor Ruth'?" she queried.

"Oh, I oughtn't to talk out of turn ..." said Toby, gathering up the plates.

"Oh no," chuckled Ron. "You don't know Tania. You won't be allowed to get away that easily. If there's one thing she can't resist, it's a mystery." He looked around the bar. "And don't pretend you've got things to do, because you're not exactly run off your feet, are you?"

"Well, I suppose ..."

"So how about if I ask you if you would bring us a couple more drinks, not forgetting one for yourself, and then you can come and sit down with us and deliver the dirt. Assuming that there is any, of course."

Toby gave a good-humoured grin. "Rather more the reverse, if truth be told. However ... just let me sort things out a sec." Within moments he had removed the remnants of the meal, seen the young couple off the premises with smiling charm, checked with the cribbage-players to make sure that their requirements were satisfied and delivered two mugs of ale to them and, armed with a tray of drinks, seated himself in the booth alongside Ron.

"So," coaxed Tania, "why 'poor Ruth'?"

"It's quite funny that you should be doing your particular play this week," replied Toby. "You know, what with the themes running through it being all about love and so on."

"How so?" Tania sounded surprised.

"Ha!" laughed Toby. "Don't think, just because I run a pub, I don't have time for the finer things in life. My Angela and I, we always make sure we go and see most of the plays down at the theatre. Regulars, we are. Except for the thing which was on last week, that is. We got the nod to stay well away from that. Doom-laden modern rubbish, that's what I was told by a certain stage manager of my acquaintance, who shall remain nameless." He gave a wink. "But Shakespeare, he's one of our favourites, and in my book, 'Midsummer Night's Dream' is one of his best. Loved it ever since I did it at school. So yes, Reuben and I had a good long chat about it when we knew you lot were coming to do it."

"And Ruth comes into this because ...?" said Ron, wondering when the landlord would come to the point.

"Well, like I say, apart from the characters which you two are playing, you've got the young lovers, who are all in a tangle. Especially the girl who's in love with the boy who's in love with someone else."

"So!" Light began to dawn in Tania's mind. "Ruth is in love with ...?" She waited expectantly.

"Matthew Sutcombe," said Toby.

After a moment's pause for the information to sink in, Ron nodded in understanding. "Simeon's ... Ah."

"As you say, 'ah'. Hence, 'poor Ruth'. The girl's head over ears, for all that she's obviously on a hiding to nothing. And it's not as if Matt's ever done the slightest thing to encourage her, for all I know. Well, he wouldn't, would he? But she fell hook line and sinker the first time she clapped eyes on him, by all accounts, and that was it. My Angela's even tried to have a quiet word with her, so it's not as if she doesn't know the score, but it was no use. It wouldn't have been so bad if she'd taken a shine to young Luke Crowan, for all that he's involved with Naomi Constantine, but no. So she's stuck mooning after Matthew, who does his best to keep out of her way, to give him his due, while Simeon makes snipey remarks on the sidelines."

Tania sighed. "Oh well. I suppose the heart wants what the heart wants, even when there's no rhyme or reason to it. But I can see why it's not exactly a happy situation."

"And it's not as if it's the only tangle going on," said Toby.

"Oh?" Tania raised encouraging eyebrows.

"Well, it's really the other side of the same coin. You see, somehow or other, Simeon got it into his head that Luke was interested in Matthew. Mad, of course, because anyone with half a brain can see that Luke's only got eyes for Naomi, but once Simeon gets an idea into his head, there's no talking sense into him. My Angela, bless her heart, even tried to pour some oil on the troubled waters and tell him it was all nonsense."

"It sounds as if your wife is very much the village peace-maker," remarked Tania. "Any luck?"

Toby shook his head. "Simeon wouldn't hear her out. He's like a dog with a bone."

"And we know what that's like," put in Ron. "We've seen Hamlet with a bone. In fact, if Ruth gets him some really good ones, he'll be her slave for life, and then ..."

"Shush, Ron," said Tania. "Enough on the subject of Hamlet and bones. This is much more interesting." She leaned forward. "Sorry, Toby. Do go on."

"Well, it's got a bit awkward. Simeon's threatened to report Luke to the police for 'inappropriate behaviour in the workplace', which to my way of thinking would be completely over the top, even if what he thinks were true. I mean, the lads are both adults, aren't they? So Naomi's up in arms about that, for all that she's very calm and easy-going usually, and that's not to mention the trouble over Simeon having a go at her about her work on one of his pet plays. Incompetent, he called her."

"Really?" Tania sounded astonished. "That doesn't sound likely. I mean, it's not as if we've had a great deal to do with Naomi, but she was telling us about her plans for the sound for our play and it all sounded excellent. And I know Leah said she was very happy with the way things went at Technical."

"Ah, well, that's your play, isn't it? I'm talking about one of Simeon's masterpieces." Toby's tone was dry in the extreme.

"What, you mean he'd written something?" queried Ron. "And it was performed here?"

"Oh no," responded Toby. "I doubt if he's got the talent to actually write a play." He chuckled. "It's a bit like what they say about teachers – you know, 'Those that can, do; those that can't, teach'. No, there was some play written by some young protégé of Simeon's from London, and Simeon directed it. Terrible dross, it was. Angela and I made the mistake of going to see it. Couldn't make head nor tail of it, and by all accounts, neither could the

100

audiences. Well, those half dozen who actually came to see it. Total disaster. But Simeon decided to put all the blame on Naomi. He said that, because of her incompetence, all the sound and lighting stopped the play's 'message' ..." Toby made air quotes with his fingers. "... getting through. He even tried to get rid of her, but luckily everybody in the group backed her up, and of course Luke leapt to her defence, and the Trustees didn't fall for it. But it didn't make him any extra friends."

"I'd imagine not," observed Ron.

"Oh dear," said Tania. "I hope we don't get any of these ructions affecting our play."

"Course you won't," replied Toby comfortingly. "All our lot are very good at their jobs, and they'll see you right. And who knows, Simeon may even stay away completely, which would be the cherry on the cake." He stood. "And speaking of which, are you sure I can't tempt you to a bit of pud? 'Cos there's one of Angela's freshly-baked cherry pies out in the kitchen, and it's just waiting for somebody to cut a couple of slices. Nice dollop of clotted cream on top? Nothing better, I reckon." He gave as enticing a smile as could be expected from a weather-beaten pirate.

Tania and Ron exchanged glances. "You win, Toby," laughed Tania. "But if my costumes end up needing to be let out, I'm blaming you."

Chapter 10
Monday

"Oh no!"

"What's up, love?" Ron poked a face half-covered in shaving foam out from the en-suite bathroom, to find Tania standing at the open wardrobe door, her handbag in her hand.

"Look at this." Tania held up the bag, which had one end of its strap hanging loose. "The stud holding the strap together has pulled out, so I can't use it. And it's my favourite bag too. It's the one you bought me for our anniversary. That's so upsetting." She looked a little tearful.

"Let me take a look." Ron emerged and took a seat on the end of the bed, holding a hand out for the bag. "Actually," he said, after a few moments' inspection, "it's nowhere near as bad as you think. See, the strap's just threaded through this ring part and then doubled back on itself and held with the stud. If you just cut off the end couple of inches, thread it back through, and then put a fresh stud in, it'll be as good as new. And you won't really lose anything, because the strap's adjustable anyway." He smiled up at his wife.

"Are you sure?"

"Positive."

"Well then, I'll just have to go and get it fixed when we're back home." Tania sighed. "What a shame. I love this bag. And I haven't brought another one, so I'm going to be a bit lost without it."

"Hold on a sec." Ron thought rapidly. "What about Reuben Hawke? I'm sure I remember seeing something about shoe repairs on his shop sign. And if he can fix shoes, then surely a bit of maintenance on a leather handbag isn't going to be beyond his capabilities."

"You think so?" A hopeful smile.

"I'd put money on it."

Tania bent down to give Ron a hug and a kiss. "You're a genius."

"I know," he laughed, standing. "But it never hurts to be reminded of the fact. And now, if that's all, I'll go and finish my ablutions, we can grab a bite of breakfast, and then we can take a saunter down the village and see if we can get your handbag problem sorted. Oh," he added over his shoulder, as he headed back into the bathroom, "and you might like to wipe some of that shaving foam off your face before we go, otherwise you will be getting some very funny looks."

*

The bell above the door of Hawke's Hardware jingled, and Reuben looked up from the till. "Good morning!" he greeted his visitors cheerily. "What can I do for you this morning?"

"I'm afraid we haven't come to buy anything," said Tania apologetically. "But we're hoping you can help us out."

"Of course, if I can. What's the problem?"

Tania produced her bag. "It's the handle on this. The strap's broken where the stud's pulled out, and I wondered if there was anything to be done."

"Easiest thing in the world," announced Reuben after a brief scrutiny. "I can trim the strap and then pop a new stud in there as quick as you like, and you'll never even know it had been done. Lovely soft leather, this strap, see, so it's flexible and easy to work with. And I bet the bag cost a pretty penny, so you don't want to lose the use of it, do you?"

"It's a shame to have to cut the end off though," said Ron. "I mean, losing the bronze terminal. The two ends of the strap won't quite match, but I don't suppose anyone will notice."

"You just leave that with me," twinkled Reuben.

103

"We like to work the odd miracle around here if we can." He disappeared behind a workbench which bore a mysterious array of key-cutting machinery and shoe-repair equipment, and in only a few minutes emerged with a smile of triumph, holding out the handbag. "There, m'lady. How's that?"

Tania looked at the bag, her face filled with delight. "Oh Reuben, that's marvellous. You can't tell there was ever anything wrong. And you've done the terminal and everything. You are clever." She gave him an impulsive kiss on the cheek.

"That's brilliant," said Ron, reaching for his wallet. "How much do I owe you?"

"Oh, there's no need for anything like that," replied Reuben, waving a dismissive hand. "On the house."

"You must let us give you something," protested Tania.

"Wouldn't hear of it." Reuben was adamant.

"I can't believe that people around here are so generous," said Tania, a small tear of gratitude appearing in the corner of her eye. "It's like yesterday, isn't it, Ron? Because we went down to the harbour yesterday, Reuben," she explained, "and we went into one of the shops, and something caught my eye, and we were going to buy it, but the woman in there insisted that I take it as a gift and wouldn't accept any money. She was a bit strange about it – she said that it would give me protection."

"Oh? Which shop was that?" enquired Reuben, intrigued.

"It was the Rock Shop," said Ron. "And I assume the woman was the one who owns it, although she never actually said. She just seemed to appear from the place next door."

Reuben chuckled. "Ah, that'll be old Demelza, right enough. So, you've met our local witch then?"

"She's actually a witch?" asked Tania, surprised.

Reuben chuckled. "Not really. Although some people do reckon she has the sight, and the kids round here certainly wouldn't ever take the risk of getting on the wrong side of her. But she's a good sort, and it may be a funny coincidence, but our fishermen always seem to come home with a good catch whenever she's seen them off of a morning."

"Well, she was very generous to us," said Ron. "And I must say, it's a refreshing change to meet people who refuse to accept payment for something. I get embarrassed if I don't pay my dues."

There was a slight pause. "Well, it's good to know that some people are like that," said Reuben. "It's a shame it's not everyone."

Tania sensed a change in atmosphere. "Why do you say that?"

"Oh, it's nothing really."

Tania was not to be deflected. "Oh come on, Reuben. You can't leave us hanging like that. Who are we talking about?" And as Reuben hesitated, "Don't tell me. It's something to do with Simeon Ashton-Rose, isn't it?"

"How did you know?" said Reuben in resigned tones.

"I can't imagine," replied Tania lightly. "Maybe I've got the sight too." She laughed. "But the thing is, we've heard so much about the man, it's not too hard to guess that, if someone's had their back put up, he's behind it." She pulled a face. "If you see what I mean."

"Come on then, Reuben," encouraged Ron. "What's he done to you? It's obviously something to do with money."

"And it's not even as if it's that much," admitted Reuben ruefully. "No, it's the principle of the thing. And you can't say the Trust is hard up, because to give him his due, Simeon's absolutely brilliant at getting all sorts of

105

grants and subsidies for the theatre from the arts people and the local authorities. I've no idea how he does it."

"Friends in high places?" suggested Tania.

"More like that he knows where the bodies are buried," said Reuben darkly. "He strikes me as the sort of chap who'd poke that long nose of his into people's business and winkle out their guilty secrets."

"Don't tell me the lovely people round here have got guilty secrets?" smiled Tania.

"Only the ones he's made up. I've heard one or two things he's said about people, which I don't believe a word of."

"So what's he done to you?" wondered Ron. "He hasn't been winkling out your guilty secrets, has he?" He laughed to make it clear that the remark was not to be taken seriously.

Reuben took a breath. "There was one of his plays. Well, not his exactly, but one written by some chum of his, which he directed here."

"I wonder if this is the same one we were hearing about before?" murmured Tania to Ron.

"Anyway, it was a right load of old tosh, from what I've been told."

"Sounds like the same one to me," muttered Ron in reply.

"I never got to see it from out front, because I was running it backstage, but that's what I heard," continued Reuben. "Actually, the one thing I never did hear was any applause. There were hardly any people in to see it, and those that did come were off like a shot at the end, almost before we'd got the front-of-house lights up so that they could see their way out. Well, as you can imagine, Simeon was not best pleased. He took it out on everyone but himself. Come the last night, there was an almighty ruckus."

"Yes, we heard he put the blame on Naomi."

"Oh, not just her. He stormed back into the props room after the play in a right tantrum, and smashed all the props that Mary had spent hours making. Said they weren't fit for a professional theatre, and they looked more like something that had been made at play school. He told her that if she was too old to make a proper job of things, she should get out and make room for someone better. She was in a bit of a state, of course, but we all rallied round afterwards and stood up for her, so it never came to anything."

"So where did you come into this?" asked Tania.

"Well, once he'd finished with the women, because he probably thought they were easier targets ..." Tania took a sharp intake of breath in outrage, but bit her lip as Reuben carried on. "... he turned his fire on me. Said the scenery that I'd put together wasn't up to scratch, and it'd completely made nonsense of the play's story. And I told him, it didn't need my scenery to do that."

"I bet that went down well," remarked Ron.

"Well, I ask you," appealed Reuben. "You get a few scribbles in crayon from this so-called playwright, for a set which is supposed to be half mental hospital ward and half Egyptian tomb, and what do you expect? I spent hours trying to make sense of it, and Mary did her best with all the bits and pieces in both settings, but nothing was good enough for his lordship. So he refused point-blank to pay a bean towards our costs. Not that either of us had spent that much, except in time scrounging stuff and trying to make a silk purse out of this pig's ear, but it rankled." Reuben let out a gusty sigh. "And then he goes and spends a load of money on getting me to order fancy wallpapers and the like so that the flat at the White House can be redecorated 'in the original spirit of the building'. And that cost a mint, I can tell you."

"Don't say he refused to pay for that as well," said Tania.

"Oh no. He paid up, at about the fourth time of asking. But it did cross my mind to wonder, whose money is he spending?"

*

The heat had gone out of the day as Ron and Tania started to make their way down Fore Street in the direction of the theatre. Debating what to do after their successful visit to the hardware shop, they had decided that they should take advantage of the continuing beautiful summer weather to do a little exploring, and a few brief moments poring over the local guide books at Hollyhock Cottage gave Tania an idea.

"Look, Ron," she said, spreading out a map. "There's a footpath leading from the top of the village near the caravan site, over the hill, to an old abandoned tin mine on the other side, which seems to be set up as some sort of heritage centre. We could walk over there, maybe get a spot of lunch, and be back in plenty of time to put our feet up before dress rehearsal this evening. What do you think?"

"A cunning plan if ever I heard one," agreed Ron. "Let me change into some better boots, and we're off."

As the couple passed the caravan park, they could hear the sound of happy childish laughter, interspersed with exuberant canine barking, filtering over the hedge. "Sounds as if David and Elizabeth are letting the boys wear themselves out," observed Tania. "Maybe that'll stop them getting over-excited this evening."

"And it seems that Peter and Martha have offloaded Hamlet with the same idea," added Ron. "Good thinking all round."

The path up and over the hill gave spectacular views out across the sea in one direction, and up towards distant tor-dotted moors in the other, before it descended into a dim tree-shaded cleft, alive with the song of birds, eventually emerging at the foot of a steep climb towards a clifftop where the finger of an old tin mine chimney pointed skywards. The couple arrived somewhat hot and breathless at the site, to find the former wheelhouse buildings in a semi-ruinous state, while an adjacent gaggle of structures had been refurbished for visitors. There was a re-creation of a tiny mine-worker's cottage, with its cast-iron range, rough pine furniture, rag rugs on the earth floor, and a box bed into which, according to the accompanying signs, a family of six would have been crammed all together. By contrast, the Master's House featured rooms with much more gracious proportions, with panelled walls, floors of wide oaken boards, furniture which aimed to follow the fashion of the times although clearly provincial in construction, and framed etched prints on the walls. An outbuilding at the back was set up as a rudimentary schoolroom, with forms in rows, chalk and slates for the pupils to copy the lessons written up on the blackboard, and a cane hanging ominously on a nearby hook for use on those who proved inattentive. And alongside the school premises was another little stone building, rough in its outward appearance but much more welcoming in its rôle as a cafe, which offered seating in its little umbrella-shaded cobbled yard, where visitors were already enjoying cups of tea, cooling drinks, and some of the most generously-filled sandwiches Ron had ever seen.

"I don't know about you, love," he said, after well over an hour had flown by unnoticed, "but I'm ravenous. It must be all that walking and fresh air. I could murder a cup of tea to start with, and then I've got my eye on one of those sarnies."

"You seem to do nothing but eat," laughingly protested Tania. "But I must confess, I agree with you. I am feeling peckish."

"Good day to you, folks," said the man behind the

tiny counter as the couple peered their way into the dimly-lit interior. "Welcome to The Piggery. What can I get you?"

"The Piggery?" echoed Tania.

"Indeed yes, ma'am. That's what this building used to be in the olden days," replied the man, his craggy elderly face seamed into a smile. "All the folks round here would keep a pig or two. Wonderful things, pigs. They ain't fussy eaters, so you can keep them going with all the peelings and leavings and any old bits of gorse and foliage during the summer, and they'll keep you going during the winter, what with the chitterlings and the brawn and the salted meat and the smoked bacon and whatnot. Did you notice the hooks in the chimney of the cottage? That's where they used to hang up a whole pig's leg to smoke."

"Er ... no, I think we must have missed that," murmured Tania faintly.

"Well, there you are," responded the man cheerfully. "So, what's it to be? Now, being as we're The Piggery, we does a house speciality of a really good bacon sammich. How about a couple of those?"

"I think perhaps we'll give those a miss," said Ron. "It would feel a bit too much like eating our hosts. So what else can you suggest that's local?"

"We does a pretty fine Ploughman's Lunch," offered the man. "Nice big chunk of wholemeal cottage loaf, which we bakes ourselves here round the back. Then you gets a piece of proper Cornish Yarg, nettles and all, and that comes with butter and pickles from the same farm up away. Proper job, it is."

"I like the sound of that," said Ron.

"Not too sure about the nettles," demurred Tania.

"Well, you got the Fisherman's Lunch, if you'd rather, miss. Same as, but with a good dollop of mackerel pâté instead of the cheese. All made fresh, 'cos my young 'un never comes back into harbour without some mackerel in amongst his catch, and his missus is a dab hand in the kitchen. How does that sound?"

Ron and Tania exchanged glances. "I think we're hooked," smiled Ron. "Can we have one of each, and a pot of tea to start with?"

"Coming right up. Get yourselves a seat, and I'll be out to you in two shakes."

"And then," remarked Tania, "I think we should probably be thinking about starting back. I'm going to want a bath and a change of clothes, and I expect you'll want to put your feet up before dress rehearsal."

"You know me so well," chuckled her husband. "Just make sure you wake me in plenty of time to get my brain in gear."

*

"So, good night unto you all.
Give me your hands, if we be friends,
And Robin shall restore amends."

The single spotlight on Susannah dimmed to darkness as she delivered Puck's closing lines, and after a moment's pause there came the sound of applause from a solitary pair of hands from the middle of the rows of seats. A few seconds later, the general lighting came up, to reveal Leah seated in the auditorium, smiling proudly as she clapped.

"Right, everyone on stage!" she commanded in ringing tones as she rose and made her way carefully down to the front of the steeply-raked stalls, and in response the cast emerged from various points around the stage, with the theatre's technical team hovering in the background. "That," she continued, "was excellent. Well done, cast. The same to you and your team, Reuben. I am delighted. And since I do not subscribe to the theory that a good first night requires a bad dress rehearsal, I have every confidence that we are in for a great success." The cast and crew exchanged smiles of pleased satisfaction. "Now ..." Leah took a look at her watch. "All I have left to do is set the curtain call ..."

There was an almost inaudible sigh of resignation from the company.

"... but in view of the hour, I don't plan to do that now." Hopeful smiles reappeared. So what I have in mind is to come back tomorrow ..." The sigh was repeated. "... not for a full rehearsal, but for a speed run. No costumes, no lighting or sound, so your team is off the hook, Reuben. I'll give notes from tonight, and then we'll just run through the lines at breakneck speed, without moves, just to cement them in your brains. After all, I can't let you have a whole day off, and then I'll set the walk-downs. With a bit of luck and a following wind, we can have the whole thing wrapped up in an hour, which will leave you all free for the rest of the day." An unexpected warm smile lit up her normally severe features. "Since I understand that there is a certain special village celebration at the pub that I'm sure nobody will want to miss. Least of all, I confess, me." A ripple of laughter. "So back here at noon, please. Thank you."

Chapter 11
Tuesday

"Good morning, Ruth!" Ron hailed the young assistant stage manager, as he and Tania came face to face with her at the top of the lane leading to the White House.

"Oh! Hello," came Ruth's rather startled response. "Sorry, I didn't notice you. I was thinking of something else."

"Gorgeous morning, isn't it?" said Tania. "We're just off to the theatre for that final run-through of the play. And what are you up to today?"

"Oh, I'm going down to the theatre as well."

"How come? Our director said yesterday that she wouldn't be needing any of the technical people today. Or did somebody have to come to let us in?"

"Oh no," replied Ruth. "The gate at the side of the White House is always unlocked, so you can all get in that way. No," she continued, holding up a large white plastic carrier bag whose evidently heavy contents, bulky and oddly-shaped, seemed to be dripping a trickle of blood from one corner. "I promised Susannah I'd meet her here. I've got some bones for her dog."

"By the look of it, Hamlet's in for a treat," commented Ron. "Your uncle obviously came up trumps." He laughed. "But I hope Peter isn't going to be letting Hamlet have one of those in the dressing-room during the performances, otherwise the audience won't be able to hear anybody's lines for the sound of crunching bones."

"I don't think we need to worry about that," remarked Tania. "I seem to remember Reuben telling us that the dressing-rooms were pretty much soundproof. No, I should think the biggest difficulty will be dragging Hamlet away if he's halfway through a bone when it's time for his entrance with us."

As the three reached the approach to the White House, Tania couldn't help but notice Ruth's eyes straying to scan the upper windows of the building, as if hoping to catch a glimpse of someone. "So," she said brightly, aiming to distract the young woman's attention, "what are your plans for today? I expect you'll be looking forward to the Feast tonight."

"Oh yes," said Ruth with enthusiasm. "Everyone is. In fact, when I've dropped these off," she continued, as the trio passed through the gate and emerged on to the house's rear terrace, "I said I'd go back and do some work for my uncle. He always makes a special batch of sausages for the Feast, so he wants me to help with those and then get them over to Toby for Angela to make her famous Mummers' sausage rolls. Then I'll be helping Toby to get the ballroom set up."

"You seem to be the maid of all work everywhere around the village, as well as in the theatre," smiled Ron.

"That's life as an A.S.M.," said Ruth, echoing the smile.

"Well, as long as you're properly appreciated." Ron couldn't help but notice that Ruth's smile became rather more strained, as she unconsciously glanced back over her shoulder up towards the White House.

"And here we are!" cried Tania, as the three descended the auditorium steps to join the company at the bottom. "And look. Ruth here has brought a treat for a certain someone."

It was obvious that the 'certain someone' already had an inkling of the treat in store, as by now Hamlet was snuffling with excitement and reaching forward, apparently attempting to pull Susannah's arm out of its socket as he strained towards the enticing odours emanating from Ruth's dripping carrier bag.

"This is all very good of you, Ruth," spoke up Leah

drily. "But I suspect that we'll get no sense out of our canine cast member for the rest of the day. However," she added, "I think we can dispense with his services for the script run, since he doesn't have very many lines, so may I suggest, Peter, that you find a convenient place to tether him and leave him to enjoy one of his bones while the rest of us get on with some actual work."

"I can do that, Leah," said Ruth hastily. "There's a metal ring I can put his lead through just at the side of the stage. And shall I put the rest of the bones in your dressing room, Peter?"

"Not if they're leaking blood," he responded. "Just leave them somewhere here where he can't see them, and I'll put them inside later."

"Oh, Yes. Right," faltered Ruth, taking Hamlet's lead from Susannah. "I'll ... er ... do that. Sorry, Leah. I didn't mean to ...," she apologised, flushing with embarrassment and fading into silence, before disappearing at the side of the stage. She reappeared a few moments later, dog-less and leaving behind her the unmistakeable sounds of strenuous gnawing, before placing the carrier bag at the foot of the central steps and then making her escape through the wings and up the narrow lane at the side of the theatre.

"And now, people," said Leah, after a long deep breath, "shall we rehearse?"

*

"I'm excited," Tania confided to Ron, as they made their way back up through the theatre in the wake of the dispersing company. "After all the to-ing and fro-ing, that's the last time we'll do our lines until we're in front of an audience. And I hope Leah's pleased."

"I think you can count on it," replied her husband. "In fact, it may be something to do with the Cornish air, but it seems to me that a total change has come over that woman."

"What do you mean?" wondered Tania.

"Oh, nothing serious," Ron reassured her in response to her furrowed brow. "But you know she's always been a stickler for doing things the traditional way. You know, never saying the last line of the play until the dress rehearsal, or not setting the curtain calls until the last minute. And most important of all, the tradition of the director never admitting that they're satisfied with what the actors are doing. But she's positively glowing." He gave a chuckle. "You don't suppose the real Leah's been kidnapped by aliens, and they've put a niced-up clone in her place?"

"Fool!" laughed Tania. She gave her husband a gentle swat of reproof, as the couple reached the top of the steps, to find the members of the Kent family clustered together waiting for them on the terrace. "Hello, you lot," she greeted them. "Did you want something?"

"Yes," replied David. "You."

"Sorry?"

"Daddy's doing a barbecue," announced Daniel importantly. "And everyone's coming."

"And you have to come too," piped up Josh, as his brothers loudly chorused "Please!"

Ron and Tania exchanged glances. "Well," laughed Ron, "in the face of such determination, I don't see how we can refuse."

"Anything to help keep the children amused," whispered Elizabeth in an aside to Tania.

"Paul and Tim said they're going to pop into the pub and see if they can scare up some tinnies from the landlord," said David.

"Now that's an idea," said Ron. "Why don't Tania and I nip back to our cottage and grab a bottle of wine, and we'll see you up at your caravan in a few minutes."

"And I hope Peter's remembering to bring along

one of his bones for Hamlet, or none of us is likely to get any barbecue at all," quipped Tania.

"Don't worry about that," said Elizabeth. "I saw him pick up the whole bagful as they were leaving."

"So that's that," added her husband. "Just follow the trail of blood drips, and that's where we'll be!"

After a very agreeable lunchtime during which, by some miracle of mutual consent, the play was hardly mentioned at all, Ron looked at his watch and nudged Tania in her adjacent deck chair. "Delightful as this has been," he said, standing, "we had better get on. We've got food to defrost for the Feast at the pub tonight. We said we'd contribute, as Toby is going to let us hold our first night party in their ballroom tomorrow night. I take it we're all going this evening?"

"Wouldn't miss it for the world," said Andrew. "It'll take our minds off wanting to go through our lines."

"And you never know," remarked Tania. "You might be able to pick up some tips on donkey behaviour from the 'Obby Ass."

There was a chorus of puzzled exclamations. "What on earth is an 'Obby Ass?" queried Andrew.

"You mean you haven't heard all about the Midsummer Mumming?" asked Ron.

There was head-shaking all round. "I haven't really had much to do with the locals," admitted David. "We thought this feast business was just some sort of party at the pub."

"I can't believe it," exclaimed Ron. "You are all in for a treat," he said, and went on to relate Toby Hayle's explanation about the revival of the ancient ritual.

"So you mean there's some sort of competition among the local lads to see who's best and bravest?" queried Paul. "I reckon I'm up for that." He elbowed Timothy. "What do you say, Tim? Shall we show these local yokels what's what?"

"Hey, don't you go leaving us out," cried James. "Tom and I can hold our own in a ruck. Well, I can, anyway."

"I'm not so sure," said Elizabeth. "I wouldn't mind betting that some of the local farmer's boys are pretty tough."

Leah stepped in. "I am not going to have any of my Rude Mechanicals put out of action by some sort of unruly horseplay," she said sternly.

"Or ass-play," murmured Ron to Tania with a grin.

"So, James and Thomas," Leah continued, "you two youngsters are firmly out of it. Paul and Timothy, on the other hand, despite all the evidence to the contrary, are adults, and can make up their own minds."

Timothy put his hand up. "I've made my mind up already. If Paul's going to get whacked, I'll just watch, thanks all the same."

"Good for you, mate," said Paul, clapping the other on the shoulder. "But it sounds like fun."

"On your head be it," said Leah. "I've had my say. And now I think I'll join Tania and Ron, and be away. And I shall see you all later." Amid a chorus of farewells, the three made their way out of the caravan park and down the lane towards the village centre, leaving the spectacle of Paul doing mock strong-man poses to the amusement of the others.

*

The noise level in the packed ballroom at the Pilchard's Arms had reached deafening levels when Toby Hayle, in his rôle as master of ceremonies, rang the lounge bar's hand-bell vigorously in order to gain attention.

"Ladies and gentlemen," he cried. "We now come to the most important part of the evening! The selection of the 'Obby Ass and the Lord of Misrule for tomorrow's Midsummer Mumming!" A resounding cheer went up.

"So, first of all, can everyone make a space in the middle of the floor, and can the candidates step forward." Amid much general jostling, the crowd cleared back towards the walls of the ballroom, and a dozen or so young men stepped forward, among them, Tania noticed to her surprise, Matthew Sutcombe.

"I say," she whispered to Mary Pengelly who happened to be standing alongside her. "I didn't expect to see him taking part. I wouldn't have thought the members of that particular household would have regarded themselves as part of village life." She nodded in the direction of Simeon Ashton-Rose, who stood aloof at one end of the room, a disdainful expression on his face as he looked down his long nose at his partner.

"I think Simeon feels more or less forced to come," murmured Mary in reply. "But actually, Matt is quite well-liked around the place. He's a pleasant enough chap, for all that he's a bit quiet, and he gets on all right with folks in his own way. For some reason, Simeon's unpopularity doesn't seem to have rubbed off on him too badly. Oh, we'd better shush," she said. "They're starting."

"Now, ladies and gents," began Toby. "First off we've got ..."

"Here, hold on a minute," cried a man at the front of the crowd. "That chap there ain't a local." He pointed to Paul, who stood among the group in the centre of the room. "He's one of these theatricals. He can't put himself up."

"Ah, now, I've been asked about this," intervened Toby. "And as far as I can tell, the rule is that the participants have to live in or around Polkernow. And although it's true, this young gentleman don't come from round here, being as how he's living in my pub for the time being, I reckon that qualifies him. Any questions?"

"Well, fair enough," conceded the man. "Let's see

how this here townie measures up to our own lads." There was a general ripple of laughter around the room.

"Right," said Toby, re-assuming control. "We're going to kick off with the Trials of Strength. You lads, split yourselves into two teams. It's time for the Tug-o'-War." Amidst much jostling, two teams formed, a sturdy rope was produced, and to the accompaniment of a great deal of vocal encouragement, and with much grunting and straining, the winning team eventually managed to pull their opponents across the chalk line drawn on the floor. But the victors had no time for self-congratulation because they, split afresh into two smaller teams, repeated the contest, until the numbers were reduced to a single contestant on either side, as Paul found himself pitted against a local young giant, well over six feet tall, with cheerful rubicund features beneath a mop of tousled dark curls. There was little doubt of the outcome, and to general acclaim Toby was able to announce, "And the winner is Adam Sennen!"

Further contests followed. Bales of straw were brought out and stacked up, with the contestants required to clear a steadily increasing height as best they could in a single vault. Then a bar was set up, similar to a high jump, over which a heavy sack had to be thrown as the bar was gradually raised, until all save one had been eliminated. The temperature in the room rose as the events progressed, until Toby rang the hand-bell once more to declare, "Now that's all the physical challenges done, ladies and gents, bar one. But to give our young men a chance to cool down and get their breath back, we're going to move on to the other side of the contest. And for this, I'm going to hand over to my lovely wife Angela."

Angela Hayle stepped up to her husband's side. "Now ladies, I think you'll agree with me that this is the most important part of the evening. Because we can't have just anyone bearing the standard as Polkernow's 'Obby Ass, can we?"

A loud chorus of "No!"

"We got to have the best-looking chap in the village. Right?"

"Yes!" was the vociferous response.

"So come on, lads – line up. It's time for the Beauty Contest!"

"If they want to cool down," cackled an old dame in a wheelchair at the front of the spectators, "they'd better get their shirts off. We want to see what we're getting." A shout of mostly female acclamation rose from the crowd.

"Old Hannah's right," chuckled Toby. "And if it ain't part of the rules, well then it ought to be. So come on, lads. Shirts off, and then you can each do your best catwalk strut for Angela and the ladies. And I'm going to leave it to them to decide who's best. Off you go!" To a tremendous cacophony of cheering, laughter, applause and catcalls, each of the contestants took a turn to parade up and down the room, until finally Toby called a halt by ringing his bell and announcing, "And my dear wife has decided that the first place goes to ... everyone!" The declaration was greeted by a mixture of laughter and good-natured booing.

"Now lastly," cried Toby, "we got the wrestling. So lads, I need you to pair up. And the first one to manage to lift both his opponent's feet off the floor, he's the one who goes through to the next round."

The contests proceeded, until only two were left – Paul, and his nemesis from the tug-of-war. The two grappled, surprisingly well-matched in spite of the apparent difference in size, until with a final huge grunt, the other young man succeeded in lifting Paul clear of the floor, to be greeted by enormous cheering. Toby stepped forward and lifted the victor's massive paw high in the air. "And the champion for the third year in a row, and this year's 'Obby Ass – Adam Sennen, from Longships Farm!" The applause was renewed, and Adam reached across to shake Paul's hand and clout him on the shoulder with a gruff "Well done, mate".

Ron went up to Paul amidst the continuing applause. "Well done," he said. "You did the Society proud."

"Oh, he did more than that," said Toby, overhearing. "Because, listen up, everybody!" The room fell silent. "Now, what's your name again, lad?"

"Paul Durham," replied the slightly surprised young man.

"Well, everyone," said Toby, "I think this young emmet here did so well, I reckon we ought to declare him official runner-up, and this year's Midsummer Mumming Lord of Misrule." After only a moment's pause, the decision was approved by resounding applause and cheering from around the room, as the members of the Ramston Dramatic Society clustered around to offer their congratulations.

"So what exactly do I have to do?" enquired Paul of Toby, as the noise began to die away.

"Oh, it's easy enough," said Toby. "You just follow the fiddler round at the head of the procession tomorrow morning carrying the official Carrot of Love. Basically, you're the sidekick of the 'Obby Ass. I'll tell you exactly what to do then while you're getting into your costume."

"There's a costume?"

"There is. Oh, don't worry – it's not like the 'Obby Ass. That's massive, and it takes a bit of wearing, I can tell you. No, it's just like the Moorish Dancers wear. It's a white linen smock and trousers, and you've got a smart top hat with ribbons."

"Hey, hang on." Paul was struck with a sudden inspiration. "I've just had the most brilliant idea. Instead of the top hat, if I'm going to be the 'Obby Ass's sidekick, why can't I wear the ass's head from the play?"

"Just a minute," interrupted Leah. "Did I hear right? You want to use Bottom's ass's head for this procession round the streets? And what if it gets damaged? What are you going to do then?"

"I promise it won't. And it'll be brilliant advertising for the play as well. Oh, go on, Leah," pleaded Paul. "Please!"

As all the others regarded her hopefully, Leah gave a sigh of resignation. "Och well, I know when I'm beaten. Very well. But if that head gets broken, I'll be cutting yours off to use in its place."

"It'll be fine," beamed a delighted Paul. "Roll on tomorrow."

Chapter 12
Wednesday

"How's the time?" Tania's voice floated anxiously down the stairs of Hollyhock Cottage.

"We're fine," Ron called back up to her. "It's only just on half past ten, and according to Toby, the Mumming doesn't kick off until eleven."

"Good."

"And it's all done down here. I've finished washing-up the breakfast things and put everything away, so there's nothing left for you to do except finish making yourself look extra gorgeous, and we'll be off."

"Thank you, kind sir," replied Tania, appearing in the kitchen doorway. "Will this do?" She gave a twirl to show off her floaty light summer dress with its printed pattern of suns and moons.

"Very appropriate," said Ron, gathering her into a quick embrace. "But I'd better not crease you too much," he added, releasing her. "I don't want to spoil the effect."

"Is the hat too much?" Tania held a floppy straw creation with a chiffon scarf tied around the crown.

"You will be the belle of the ball," her husband assured her. "Now, let's be on our way."

"Sorry I took so long getting ready," apologised Tania, "but I'd lost track of time, and I couldn't find my phone. I think I must have put it down somewhere ..."

"Like here?" tutted Ron, picking it up from the shelf of the kitchen dresser. "So, see? Ten thirty-three. Tuck it safely away in that freshly-repaired handbag of yours, and we'll go. Time we weren't here."

The road down to the Pilchard's Arms was already beginning to be lined with people, as the number of villagers standing at their front gates was being swelled by crowds of tourists streaming down from the direction of the car park at the top of the village, while the verges

124

of the side lanes were filling rapidly with parked vehicles.

"Simeon's not going to be too chuffed if his front grass gets cluttered up with cars," remarked Ron. "Remember how annoyed he got when Leah parked her van there."

"I refuse to let the day be spoilt by thoughts of Simeon," retorted Tania. "He can be miserable if he wants to. I'm just here to have a good time, and I expect everyone else is too."

"Good point, love. Let's enjoy the fun."

It seemed, as the couple arrived in front of the pub, that the fun was already under way. A hubbub of voices arose from the crowd, while the squeals of excited children racing hither and thither filled the air. The group of Moorish dancers, ribbons floating and bells jingling, seemed to be having a last-minute rehearsal on one side of the road, while on the other, at the foot of the pub's entrance steps, surrounded by a smiling group of Ramston players, stood Paul, bursting with pride, resplendent in his dazzling white Lord of Misrule outfit, Bottom's donkey headdress rising above the throng and making it easy to spot him.

Ron and Tania pushed their way to the front of the group. "Paul, you look magnificent," declared Ron, shaking him warmly by the hand.

"As long as he doesn't start getting ideas above his station," remarked Leah, who was standing alongside. "Don't forget, you're not the star in this production."

"Oh, I'm quite used to playing second lead, Leah," laughed Paul. "I'm just going to enjoy myself while everyone else does all the hard work."

"And mind you take care of that ass's head," Leah warned him. "Woe betide you if anything happens to it after all the effort that's gone into making it."

"I shall be super-careful," Paul reassured her. "And

I'll make sure it goes safely back in its place in the props room when we're all finished."

"Good."

"And if anyone comes too near, I shall smite them with my Carrot of Love," he laughed, brandishing the two-foot-long bright orange wooden object in his hand. "That's if it can be spared, on account of the fact that I have to make sure that all the village maidens get the opportunity to kiss it." He looked around the group surrounding him. "Anyone want the chance to get in ahead of the crowd? Sarah? Esther?" He waved the carrot in their direction.

"Don't you bring that thing anywhere near me," protested Esther.

"Funny. That's not what you usually say," riposted Paul, provoking laughter all round, as the young woman blushed furiously and did her best to melt into the encircling throng.

"That's certainly the biggest carrot I've ever seen," observed Ron solemnly to the Kent triplets, who immediately went off into fits of helpless giggles.

At that moment, Toby Hayle emerged from the front door of the Pilchard's Arms, bell in hand, and set up a resounding clanging to settle the crowd. "Ladies and gentlemen!" he cried. "The time had come to begin the Midsummer Mumming!" A cheer arose. "So may I present to you the victor in this year's competition – our very own Adam Sennen as the 'Obby Ass!" With a sweeping gesture, he indicated the double gates at the side of the pub, which swung open to reveal the 'Obby Ass in all its glory. Standing at least eight feet tall, the creature's head towered over the crowd, with Adam's face just visible through an opening in the neck, while the ribbons festooning the body swirled and danced as the wearer twisted and curvetted. There was an enthusiastic hurrah, as Toby began to marshal the procession into some sort of order. First, the ancient fiddler sprang into position at its head and began to caper with surprising agility, with Paul stationed immediately behind him. Then the 'Obby Ass took position, while the Moorish dancers formed up at the rear. When everybody was in place, Toby consulted his watch, rang his bell once more, and called for silence. There was widespread shushing, and the church clock could be heard chiming the quarters. Then, on the first stroke of eleven, there was an explosion of cheering, the fiddler struck up, and they were off.

Down Fore Street they went to great acclaim, with giggling girls being pushed to the front of the crowd as Paul, with evident great enjoyment, presented the Official Carrot to be kissed by those who wished to find their true love. As he passed Tresillian's butcher's shop, where the family stood on the threshold, Tania from her place in the following throng was intrigued to see Ruth being encouraged by her relatives to take part in the ritual, despite her evident reluctance. There was no such reluctance a little further down the street, where the front garden wall of a row of ancient almshouses was lined with the residents, mostly elderly women, among them the old lady in the wheelchair who had been so vociferous at the parade of young men at the previous evening's Feast. Each of the ladies was insistent on taking her turn to kiss the Carrot, to universal merriment, before the parade passed by. And as the sun rose higher in a cloudless sky, the entire village echoed to the sounds of innocent celebration.

*

To the chimes of St. Petroc's church clock striking quarter to seven, as they passed the Pilchard's Arms on their way to the theatre, Tania and Ron were joined by Andrew and the other four young actors as they emerged from the pub.

"We'd better hurry," said Tania. "Leah said she

127

wanted everyone there well before seven for some reason, so we're going to be late."

"We won't be the only ones," said Sarah. "Look, Leah's only just ahead of us." She pointed to the figure of the director, who was just turning the corner into the lane leading to the theatre. "And see, the Kents are only just coming down the hill, so I think we'll be all right."

"It's just that I hate to be in a rush before the first performance," replied Tania. "I like time to get settled."

"You'll be fine, love," Ron reassured her. He turned to Paul. "So, how are you feeling after all your exertions this morning?"

"Terrific!" grinned Paul. "I haven't enjoyed myself so much in ages. I could do it all again tomorrow."

"I don't know if Leah would approve. She's very protective of Bottom's ass's head."

"Then I've got nothing to worry about," said Paul confidently. "I made sure I put it back safe and sound in its place in the props room as soon as this morning's parade was over, so there's no reason why I shouldn't be in her good books. And I told everyone I met to make sure they came to see the play this week, so gold star for me, I think."

The group were met at the front door of the White House by Luke Crowan, who beckoned them into the building with a smile. "Come on in, everyone," said the front-of-house manager. "No need to go down to your dressing rooms just yet. We suggested to your director that she call you all a little before the usual half-hour before curtain-up, because we always arrange a little get-together up here first." He ushered the group into the cafe area, to join the rest of the cast and crew who were standing about chatting, with the exception of Simeon Ashton-Rose, who stood aloof in one corner, a pinched expression on his face, alongside Matthew Sutcombe.

Leah looked at the new arrivals and clapped her

hands for silence. "Is that the last of us? Good. Now, ladies and gentlemen, I've been told that the tradition here at the Mandyke Theatre is for the management to hold a small reception of welcome on the first night of a visiting group's performances." A murmur of surprised pleasure. "But first, I believe the theatre's artistic director wants to say a few words." She held out an arm to give Simeon the floor. "Mr Ashton-Rose?"

Simeon stepped forward. "I simply wished to offer you the theatre's good wishes, and to express the hope that you will rise to meet our exceptional standards. I shall be watching to ensure that you do."

After a slightly uncertain pause, there was a ripple of muted applause, and Reuben Hawke spoke up. "So that's it, ladies and gentlemen. Feel free to tuck in. It's nothing too extravagant – just a cup of tea and a few little sandwiches and cakes, which our friendly cafe hostess Judith Polkerris has supplied out of the kindness of her heart. And you'd best not waste time," he added with a chuckle. "I shall be giving you your half-hour call in just ..." He consulted his watch. "... thirty-one minutes."

The company needed no further invitation, and Judith and her sister Mary Pengelly were kept busy dispensing the refreshments, with Naomi Constantine and Luke handing out drinks, while Ruth Tresillian and Reuben cleared away empty plates and cups. Soon people were dotted about the room eating, drinking, and chatting, and Tania found herself standing next to Matthew, who had become separated from Simeon. She gave him a friendly nod. "Did you enjoy yourself at the Feast last night?" she enquired. "Hard luck on not winning, but I thought you did very well."

"Oh, I never expected to win," replied Matthew with a blush and a surprisingly sweet smile. He gestured to himself. "I mean, this isn't exactly a Mr Universe body, is it? But some of the local guys talked me into it. Simeon disapproved horribly, of course, but I think it's fun to be part of the village activities sometimes. The people round here are mostly a pretty friendly bunch, even though there aren't that many who get on with Simeon."

"I've noticed that he isn't exactly popular," remarked Tania delicately.

"They don't know him properly," Matthew stoutly defended his partner. "There's a lot of good in him really."

'Deep down, obviously,' Tania thought to herself, and decided to change the subject. "And it was a lovely surprise to find all this when we got here. We've already enjoyed some of Judith's food when we went to her cafe for cream teas the other day."

"I hope you ate your scones the proper Cornish way," smiled Matthew. "You know, jam first and then cream. That's one of the first things I had to learn when I came down here. If you do it the wrong way round like they do in Devon, cream first and jam afterwards, the food police throw you out of the county and back over the Tamar." He laughed.

"Thank goodness we got it right first time." Tania joined in the laughter. "Anyway, I can't imagine Judith doing anything so unkind as throwing anybody out of anywhere. If this little tea party is anything to go by, she seems a very generous woman."

"And most people would agree with you," said Matthew. His brow darkened. "Although some wouldn't."

"Really?" Tania's raised eyebrows invited Matthew to proceed.

"Oh, it was all rubbish really," said Matthew. "But there was a point when the takings of the bar and cafe here took a dip, for no reason that anyone could understand. And Simeon took it into his head to accuse Judith of siphoning off the profits here to support her own teashop. Nobody believed it, of course, but she was so upset by the accusation, it's a wonder she didn't just walk away from the theatre and leave Simeon to get on with it. But her sister told him where to get off, and said that if he wasn't careful, everybody would leave and he'd be high and dry, so eventually he backed down. But it caused a lot of bad feeling."

"I can imagine."

"Anyway, I'd better get back to Simeon. He's looking over this way, and nobody's talking to him, so I can't just leave him standing there." Matthew gave a farewell bob of the head and made his way across the room to his partner.

The general conversation around the room was interrupted by Luke Crowan, who called for everyone's attention. "I know Reuben is about to make the half-hour call, and as he's a stickler for punctuality, I just want to make a quick announcement. Which is that, as of this afternoon, your play is a complete sell-out! The box office has achieved wonders, and there's not a single ticket left!"

There was a cheer of jubilation from the entire company, and in the silence which fell as it died away, Simeon could be heard to hiss at Matthew, "Good to know that you're capable of doing your job properly sometimes at least."

The remark provoked a sudden hush, into which Matthew replied, "I don't know what you're talking about."

"You'll gladly push the tickets for some populist pot-boiler," continued Simeon in venomous tones, while everyone else in the room tried desperately to look the other way. "But when it comes to one of my plays, it's obviously another story."

"Oh, you mean that last one of yours?" Matthew laughed derisively. "Nobody in their right mind could have pushed tickets for that. It was rubbish from start to finish. I was embarrassed even to give the tickets away."

"How dare you!"

The slap sounded like a whip-crack in the silence of the cafe, and all present stared in horror at the swiftly reddening hand-print on Matthew's face, before he turned and walked unsteadily from the room.

After a moment of shocked stillness, Reuben stepped forward. "Ladies and gentlemen!" he announced loudly. "This is your half-hour call! Please make your way down to the dressing rooms. We shall be starting to admit the audience in five minutes!"

*

"Are you absolutely sure that you don't want us to help you and Angela finish clearing up?" asked Tania.

"Wouldn't hear of it," replied Toby Hayle robustly, eyes twinkling.

"Because it was our idea to have an after-show party," persisted Tania, looking around the ballroom of the Pilchard's Arms, where she and Ron were the only remaining members of the 'Midsummer Night's Dream' company left. "Everybody else has escaped, and it doesn't seem fair to leave all the work to just you two."

"What about Andrew? He's staying here, and he only left a couple of minutes ago. Surely he hasn't gone to bed yet. And Paul and Tim and the girls have only just this second gone up," pointed out Ron. "We could enlist their help."

Tania laughed. "If you think I'm going up and knocking on their doors to reveal the unsavoury truth of who's sleeping with whom, you're very much mistaken. No, we'll pitch in. It can't take that long."

"Now be off with you," retorted Toby. "If I remember right, it was me that offered to hold your little soirée here, and besides, there isn't that much to do, and my Angela and I are quite used to it." He nodded in the direction of his wife, who could be seen wrangling an armful of black bin-bags out towards the stairs. "No, I reckon you've all done quite enough work today, what with the play and the Mumming and all, so you can go and get some well-earned rest. But I hope you had a good time."

"Oh yes. With all of it," beamed Tania. "The Mumming was just a riot, and I don't expect Paul will ever stop talking about his part in it."

"And as for the play, it was just too good to be true," added Ron. "The whole thing went like a dream ..."

"Oh, very good!" guffawed Toby.

"Sorry, didn't mean to say that," apologised Ron. "But the audience was just amazing. I thought they'd never stop applauding. And Leah couldn't have been happier."

"No, I could tell that from her little speech tonight," said the landlord.

"And then the party here was just the icing on the cake," said Tania. "I think everyone had a good time."

"I hope you've got a load of photos," remarked Ron. "We can put some up on the Society's Twitter page."

Tania's face fell. "I'm so sorry, Ron. I haven't got any at all. I haven't got my phone with me. I left it in the dressing room in the rush to get up here and set things up."

Ron sighed. "Oh well. I dare say some of the others have taken pictures. We'll check in the morning. And we can pop down and collect your phone then."

"Oh, I don't know," demurred Tania. "I'd rather do it now. I don't like being without it."

"This from a woman who's forever leaving it about the place," smiled Ron in an aside to Toby. "But okay, love. We'll go down and retrieve it now, if that's what you want, even though it's the dead of night." He looked at his watch. "Although ... actually, Toby, don't I remember that the village street lights go out at midnight?"

"They do at that. Some daft economy measure by the local council," scoffed Toby. "But I don't reckon you have to worry about that." He gestured towards one of the ballroom's tall windows. "See that full moon. It'll be like daylight out there. You'll be fine."

"That's settled then," said Tania. She linked her arm through Ron's. "Shall we go?"

"Well, what husband could resist the invitation to a moonlit stroll with his wife?" grinned Ron, and with brief farewells to Toby and Angela, the couple were soon standing at the foot of the pub's entrance steps. And as they did so, just as Ron had foreseen, the lamps along Fore Street clicked off.

"Toby was right," said Tania, as the two started in the direction of the theatre, after a few moments to allow their eyes to adjust. "It's amazingly bright out here."

"Clear country air," replied Ron. "Not that mucky stuff that we get polluting the atmosphere in town."

The moon shone from a clear sky adorned with just a few threads of cloud whose gleaming edges seemed to emphasise the contrast between the brightness of the moon's face and the velvety blackness behind it. The gentle light cast a romantic silver sheen on the buildings of Polkernow, where the occasional glow from behind curtained cottage bedroom windows provided jewel accents of ruby and gold. Tania and Ron turned the corner into the lane leading to the White House, which stood like a shadowy cliff silhouetted against the sky behind, and then made their way through the gate at the side of the building and on to the rear terrace. A solitary dim light gleamed from one of the windows in the upper floor of the building behind them, and Tania held a finger to her lips, enjoining Ron to silence in order not to attract attention. Suddenly, as she turned to begin the descent to stage level, she caught her breath.

"Oh my god, Ron!" she gasped. "Look!"

At the foot of the central steps, right at the front of the stage, lay a crumpled white-clad figure. There seemed something odd about it, and as the couple began to stumble down the steps, Tania caught Ron's arm. "Oh no," she faltered. "That's Bottom's ass's head he's wearing. Oh, please ... don't let it be Paul."

"Let me," said Ron, and moved ahead of his wife to kneel alongside the figure, which lay half on its side. As he looked more closely, he could see that the clothing was not the white linen suit which had formed Paul's Mumming costume, but silver-grey silk pyjamas, and that the feet were shod, not in stout boots, but in black leather slippers. He gently rolled the figure over, hoping to check for signs of life, and gingerly lifted the mask away, to reveal the slack-mouthed features and sightless eyes of Simeon Ashton-Rose. Looking down, he was shocked to see, protruding from the chest and surrounded by staining blood, the bronze feather, Quince's prop from the play. Swiftly he checked for a pulse, but found none.

"Is he ...?" quavered Tania.

"Dead," responded Ron heavily. He looked up at his wife. "Ill met by moonlight, Tania."

Chapter 13
Thursday

"What should we do?" whispered Tania.

Ron straightened up. "We must call the police. Straight away."

"Of course. My phone's in the dressing room. I'll go and get it."

Tania made to head for the entrance to the backstage corridor, but Ron caught her arm to forestall her. "No!" he said. "You can't go back there. You never know ..." His words died as he scanned their surroundings.

"You mean you think ...?"

"I don't know what to think," replied Ron. He looked around warily. "All I know is that, whatever's happened here, the less we do, the better."

"But what about the police? Should we go up to the White House to call them?"

Ron thought for a moment. "No. Best not. We don't know the situation up there. I think one of us should go up to the village police house and rouse Constable Polkerris. We'll put the whole thing in his hands, and then he can take the next steps, whatever they are. But I don't think we ought to just leave the place deserted. So you go, and I'll stay here with the ... with Simeon."

"But ... I'll have to go past the White House. What if ...?"

"You don't need to," stated Ron. "Go out through the wings and up the side lane. It'll be just as quick, and you won't have to touch the top gate or anything. You know, just in case." He didn't elaborate.

"Okay." Tania took a deep breath. "I'll be as quick as I can." And she was gone.

It seemed to Ron to take forever, as he sat in the silence of the deserted theatre, ears pricked, alert for the slightest sound. But eventually, the pulsing blue light and the sound of a car engine heralded the arrival of Ben Polkerris, who strode though the side entrance and on to the stage area, powerful torch in hand, with Tania in his wake.

The village constable stood for a few seconds looking down at Simeon. "Well," he said with a deep sigh, "I won't ask what's all this then. It seems pretty clear. But I suppose I'd best check." He knelt alongside Simeon and held a finger to the pulse point in his neck. "It seems you weren't wrong, sir. He's dead all right. Now, questions to be asked. Have you touched him?"

"Only to roll him over," said Ron. "To see if I could help him."

"What about that there?" Ben pointed to the ass's head.

"I took it off to see who it was," explained Ron. "We didn't know. We were afraid it might be one of our friends. But then we could see that it was Simeon. And then I noticed the feather thing ..." He indicated the bronze quill impaling the dead man's chest.

Ben got slowly to his feet. "Right. Well, I'd be grateful if you two would step aside for a moment. I have to call this in." He made his way to the centre of the stage and pressed a button on a communications unit mounted on the front of his tunic. "Control? P.C. Polkerris here at Polkernow. We've got an incident ... At the Mandyke Open-air Theatre ... We'll need a unit here. Forensics too ... Because I've got a chap lying here dead, that's why ... Okay. Polkerris out." He turned to Tania and Ron. "And now we wait."

*

It seemed surreal to sit in the moonlit silence, but eventually the sound of an approaching two-tone police siren could be heard. A few moments later, a burly businesslike man in his forties appeared at the side of the stage and strode forward, torch in hand.

"Right, constable." A curt nod from the newcomer to the local officer. "What have we got?"

"A body's been discovered, sir," began Ben Polkerris, indicating Simeon's sprawled form.

"I can see that, man," barked the other. "When? Who by?"

"Perhaps the lady and gentlemen had better explain for themselves, sir," replied the constable, beckoning Tania and Ron forward from the front row of the theatre seating where they had been instructed to wait. "Mr and Mrs Faye, sir."

The new arrival looked the couple up and down. "Detective Inspector Tregarth," he announced, with a cursory flash of his identification. He did not offer to shake hands. "So, how did this come about?" he demanded.

Ron stepped forward. "I'm Ron Faye," he said, "and this is my wife Tania. We're both members of the Ramston Operatic And Dramatic Society. We've come down to perform a play at the theatre this week. 'A Midsummer Night's Dream', actually. Shakespeare, obviously." He halted, conscious that he was babbling.

"Oh, that's you, is it? I saw the billboard when we came into the village. Don't go in much for theatre, myself," remarked the inspector. "Enough drama and fairy tales in my job as it is."

Ron forbore to rise to the comment. "Our first night was tonight," he pressed on, "and we had a small party up at the village pub after the show, and we were just finishing when my wife realised that she had left something behind at the theatre."

Tania took up the tale. "I'd forgotten my phone. I'd left it in my dressing room down here," she explained. "So we decided to come down to retrieve it. But when we arrived, we found Simeon lying here, so I went up to tell

Constable Polkerris straight away."

"So this is Simeon, is it?" enquired Tregarth. He took a slow calculating look at the body.

"That's right, sir," said Ben. "Simeon Ashton-Rose. He's the boss of the theatre."

"Is he, indeed? And this was when?" resumed the inspector.

"We left the Pilchard's Arms to come down here at pretty much exactly twelve o'clock," replied Ron.

"So," said Tregarth in disbelieving tones, "you took it into your heads to go wandering about the village at midnight, when the whole place is as black as the devil's ar... ... armpit."

"It's actually quite bright in the moonlight, once your eyes get used to it," pointed out Tania hesitantly.

"Hmmm." Tregarth did not sound convinced. "So, you got here and found this Simeon chap? Exactly as he is?"

"Not quite," admitted Ron. "I did turn him over to see if I could help him, but once I saw he was dead, I didn't touch him any more. And we've touched nothing else since. Well, other than the head, of course," he added.

"What were you doing touching his head?" demanded the inspector.

"Um ... not his. I mean the ass's head." Ron gestured to the prop lying nearby. "He was ... he was wearing it when we found him."

Tregarth's face wore an expression of incomprehension. "Why on earth was he doing that?"

Tania shrugged. "We don't know. But then we saw the ..." She pointed to the bronze feather embedded in Simeon's chest. "We wondered if he might have accidentally ..." Her voice petered out.

The detective bent to examine the quill. When he arose, his face was grim. "And what exactly is that?"

"It's one of our props. We use it in the play," said Tania helplessly. "I mean, not me. One of the others."

"But not this Simeon chap?"

"No."

Tregarth made another considered inspection of the corpse. "And did you see anyone else about?" he queried.

The couple both shook their heads. "Nobody," stated Ron.

"So what was he doing here? Where did he come from?"

"If I may, sir," intervened Ben. "He lives in that big house up on the top there." He pointed.

"On his own?"

"No, sir. There's ... there's another gentleman who lives there. Mr Sutcombe." Ben did not elaborate.

"Any sign of him?"

"No, sir."

"Right." Tregarth paused in thought for several moments, before raising his voice. "Sergeant Mitchell!"

"Here, sir," replied a younger man who had appeared unnoticed behind the inspector.

"Can we get some floodlights or something rigged up here? I can't be expected to stumble about in the pitch dark, and SOCO ought to be here soon. They'll need to see what they're about."

"I may be able to sort something out, sir," volunteered Ben. "I think I may know where to find the lighting controls. See, my wife works here, and I've helped out around the place from time to time, so I reckon ..."

"Do it." Tregarth cut him off in mid flow. "Go with him, sergeant. Make sure nothing is disturbed. If this is an accident, I'm a Dutchman. For now, I'm calling this whole place a crime scene until SOCO tell me otherwise." He turned to Ron and Tania. "Right, you two. Show me exactly how you came to be here."

"Can I just get my phone first?" pleaded Tania. "Only I'm lost without it. It's in my place in dressing room 'A'."

"I know where that is, sir," said Ben. "I could get it for the lady."

"Oh, very well," assented the inspector grudgingly. "Let Sergeant Mitchell have it. But touch nothing else," he instructed.

"Right you are, sir." The two officers disappeared towards the backstage corridor.

As Tania and Ron led the way back up the steep central steps, the inspector at their heels, the theatre's general lighting came on with a muted thud.

"Now at least we can see what we're about," commented Tregarth, as the three reached the terrace at the rear of the White House. "So, tell me what happened."

"We came through that gate there." Ron pointed to the side entrance to the terrace. "And then when we got here, we looked down and ... well, there he was," he finished simply. "Just a white shape."

"And we were afraid it was one of our friends," added Tania, and was rewarded with a quizzical look from the inspector. "Oh, just some silliness from this morning," she said, flustered. "Nothing to do with Simeon. It would take too long to explain. But anyway, we hurried down, and we've told you what happened then."

Tregarth turned from looking down at the now-illuminated stage area below to survey the rear of the house. "And he lives here?" He grunted. "Lived, that is. And from what he was wearing, he must have come out of the house." He took a closer look at one of the French windows, which could be seen to be fractionally ajar. "This way, by the look of it." He glanced upwards to where the light was showing through the upstairs

141

curtains. "From there, perhaps?"

"That's his flat. And that must be his bedroom," guessed Tania. "Because he came out of there on to the balcony early the other morning, and he was wearing his dressing gown. In fact, there was a bit of a row."

"Really?" enquired the inspector, eyebrows raised.

"He was annoyed because one of us had parked in the wrong place," said Ron.

Tregarth sighed. "Not much of a motive for murder. If it was, we'd have dead traffic wardens all over the county in the holiday season. So, the constable says there's some other chap living here."

"Yes. Matthew Sutcombe," said Tania. "He's Simeon's partner."

"What, his business partner?" queried the detective.

Ron took a breath. "Just 'partner'," he said.

Tregarth showed no reaction. "I see. So, where is he, I wonder? Let's see if we can find out." Using a blue plastic glove from his pocket, he pushed open the French window and made his way indoors. "And you two. I don't want you wandering about. You can stick with me."

The interior of the building was in darkness, with just enough light filtering in from outside to show the open doorway from the cafe area to the entrance hall. The inspector led the way into the hall and found the light switch at the foot of the stairs, turning it on and suddenly filling the space with illumination, harsh after the soft moonlight outside. "Hello!" he called in a loud voice. "Police! Is there anybody here?" A pause. "Hello! Police!"

After a few moments, muffled sounds could be heard, accompanied by vigorous yapping, and a door opened on the landing above, to reveal Matthew Sutcombe pulling on a towelling robe. He blinked in the bright light of the hall. "What's going on? Who is it?" He focussed on the group below. "Tania? What are you doing here? What is this?"

Tregarth stepped forward and produced his warrant card. "Detective Inspector Tregarth of the County Police, sir," he declared. "And you are ..."

"Matthew Sutcombe. I live here. Tania, what's going on?" he appealed, closing the door carefully to shut out the continuing barking behind him.

"Oh Matt. It's Simeon." Tania stopped as words failed her.

"You want Simeon? Well, he's in here. In our ... in the bedroom." Matt crossed the landing and opened the door to what was evidently the main bedroom at the back of the house. Looking inside, he stopped abruptly. "I mean ... he should be." He looked down at the others, seemingly baffled. "Where is he?"

"Could you come down, sir?" instructed Tregarth calmly. "We'd like a word." As Matt descended the stairs, the inspector led the way back into the cafe, where he found a switch and flicked on the lights. "Perhaps you'd better take a seat, sir," he suggested, indicating chairs at one of the tables, and Matt obeyed, a look of puzzlement on his face, while Tania and Ron seated themselves alongside. "Do I understand correctly that you and Mr ..." The detective took a swift look at his notebook. "... Mr Ashton-Rose are in a relationship?"

Matt nodded. "That's right."

"Then I'm sorry to have to tell you, sir," continued Tregarth, as Tania quietly reached out and took Matt's hand, "that the gentleman has been found dead."

For a moment, it seemed as if Matt couldn't quite take in the information. "But ... dead?"

"I'm afraid so. This lady and gentleman inform me that they discovered him down on the stage of the theatre just after midnight."

Matt looked from the inspector to Tania and back

143

again. "But why would he be down there at that time of night?"

"I was hoping you might be able to tell me that, sir."

"I … I have no idea."

"Perhaps you'd like to give me an account of the last time you saw Mr Ashton-Rose, sir," requested Tregarth.

Matt appeared to be collecting his thoughts. "About eleven or so, I suppose. We'd got back from the after-show party at the pub …"

"That was the one I was telling you about, inspector," put in Ron.

"… and we went to bed shortly after that." Matt seemed to hesitate. He appeared embarrassed.

"Would that have been together, sir?" Tregarth kept his voice neutral.

"Usually, yes, inspector. We share a room."

"The one you looked into, sir?"

"Yes."

"Usually, you say? But not tonight? Why would that have been, sir?" enquired the inspector silkily.

Matt sighed. "We'd had a row earlier. Hours earlier, I mean. Before tonight's show."

"And the nature of this row, sir?"

"Oh, it was stupid. It was just about ticket sales. It didn't really mean anything. It was just Simeon having one of his strops. But there was still an atmosphere when we got home tonight, so I decided to sleep in the guest bedroom."

"The room you came out of?"

"That's right."

"And did you see or hear anything after you'd retired to this guest bedroom, sir? Any movement about the house, or any voices?"

"Not a thing, inspector. But then, I probably wouldn't anyway." Tregarth raised quizzical eyebrows. "I

144

sleep wearing earplugs. Simeon snores." Matt took a deep gulp of air. "I mean, snored." He buried his face in his hands. "Oh god."

After a pause, Tania enquired gently, "So what happens now, inspector? I mean, Matt surely can't stay here tonight after all this?"

"Indeed not, madam," replied the detective. "My Scene of Crime Officers will need to examine these premises as well as the theatre area."

"Crime?" Matt's head shot up. "What crime? Are you telling me that Simeon was ...?"

"Too early to form judgements, sir," Tregarth forestalled him.

Matt stood. "Can I see him?"

The inspector shook his head. "Not at present, sir. I can't have anyone potentially contaminating the scene until my officers have finished their work. And as for the lady's question ..."

"Some of our cast are staying at the pub in the village," said Ron. "Why can't Matthew come with us? I'm sure Toby Hayle can find a room for him. And we've got a cottage just up the road."

Tregarth thought for a moment. "That seems not unreasonable, sir. As long as you remain there. We may well wish to speak to you again. So please wait here for a moment. I'll get my sergeant to come up to accompany you while you get some things together, Mr Sutcombe, and then he can escort the three of you to the pub." He made his way out on to the White House's rear terrace, where he could be heard summoning his junior colleague, as the other three remained in the cafe, exchanging looks of speculation.

Chapter 14
Thursday

"I have no idea what happens next," said Ron, as he deposited a cup of tea at Tania's bedside at seven a.m.

*

The couple, under Sergeant Mitchell's watchful eye, had accompanied Matthew to the Pilchard's Arms where, after a few brief explanatory words to Toby Hayle, the young man had been enveloped in Angela's motherly embrace and led away to a bedroom, holding in his arms his hastily-collected dog.

"The inspector's going to want to speak to everyone involved with this play of yours," said the sergeant.

"Not now, surely?" protested Tania. "It's the middle of the night."

"You don't know my guv'nor," replied Mitchell with a grim smile. "But no, he's not that bad. But you can bet he's going to be on the tail of the forensics people to give him chapter and verse on whatever they can before any of them have the chance to get to their beds tonight. I reckon I'm in for a long one. But he doesn't spare himself either. He'll be up and at it again first thing in the morning. And he'll want everyone on parade. Although I'm not sure how we're going to get in touch with them all."

"I can help with that," suggested Tania. "That is, if you've got my phone, sergeant."

"Right here." Mitchell dived into a pocket and handed Tania's mobile over.

"What if I contact our director and tell her what's happened? She's got everyone on her phone, because we've got a contacts group for the play. And Mr Hayle here can tell you all about the local people who are involved with the theatre."

146

"I can that, sergeant," confirmed Toby from the sidelines. "And if you want them all gathered in one place, you might as well use our ballroom. It's upstairs."

"That would be very helpful, Mr Hayle," said Mitchell. "So I'll pass that suggestion back to my guv'nor, and he'll be in touch with you, Mrs ...?"

"Faye."

"Right. So if I can just get your number ..." The sergeant fished his own phone from his pocket and keyed in Tania's number. "And this is mine." He recited the details. "Call me. And now I'd better get back." The pub door closed behind him.

*

"I'll tell you what happens next," said Tania, struggling into a more upright sitting position and reaching for her phone. "I break the news to Leah and then, in all probability, all hell breaks loose." She dialled. "Hello, Leah. It's Tania. Sorry to disturb your beauty sleep at this ungodly hour, but I'm afraid I've got some bad news."

"Don't tell me," croaked the voice at the other end of the phone. *"The morning papers have arrived, and we've got a bad review."* A smoky chuckle.

"I wish it was only that, but I'm afraid it's much worse." Tania took a deep breath. "Simeon Ashton-Rose is dead."

"WHAT?" All trace of humour vanished from Leah's voice.

"Ron and I popped down to the theatre last night after the party because I'd left my phone in the dressing room," explained Tania. "And we found him lying on the stage. The police came, and they say that they're going to want to see everyone connected with the play this morning."

"But how ... I mean, who ..." Leah seemed to be struggling to come to terms with the news. *"You mean*

147

they think there's been some funny business going on? And what about the play? What are we supposed to do now?"

"They didn't seem that interested."

"Oh really?" Leah's tone was grim. *"I'll give them 'not interested'. Who's in charge?"*

"There's a detective called Inspector Tregarth. I'm supposed to call his sergeant to organise things."

"You do that, dearie. You tell him to point this inspector chap in my direction, and I'll have a wee word with him on the subject of organisation."

"I'll give him your number," said Tania, "and Toby Hayle has said we can have the meeting in the pub ballroom."

"Good. You better call this sergeant of yours. And watch out for a group message from me. I'm not going to let all our hard work go to waste, just because of the untimely demise of some puffed-up pseudo-intellectual!" Click.

"From what I could hear, that sounded like fun," observed Ron wryly.

"She's pretty steamed," agreed Tania. "Although she doesn't seem too fussed about Simeon."

"Well, it's not as if he exactly endeared himself to her," pointed out Ron. He thought for a moment. "You don't suppose she ... no, of course not. That would be ridiculous."

"What, killed him?" Tania's laugh expressed utter incredulity. "Don't be daft. Leah would never do a thing like that."

"Well," responded Ron sombrely, "Inspector Tregarth seems to think somebody did."

*

A hush fell over the ballroom of the Pilchard's Arms as, a few moments after ten o'clock, Inspector Tregarth strode into the room, Sergeant Mitchell at his heels, with Constable Polkerris bringing up the rear,

148

looking as if he desperately wished he were somewhere else. The message sent out by Leah an hour earlier had left no room for misunderstanding – all members of the Ramston theatre group were to present themselves at the stated venue for ten o'clock sharp, under pain of her most severe displeasure. The requirement from the police authorities to do so was mentioned, but treated as something of an inconvenient coincidence. And as Toby Hayle had pointed out to Ron and Tania in an undertone as the group was assembling, it had not taken a great deal of effort on his part to summon those of the villagers who were involved with the production – once Ben Polkerris had explained to his wife the reason for his midnight call to duty, and as soon as Judith had communicated the details to her sister Mary Pengelly, the word had spread in minutes. Now, the Ramston company were grouped together on one side of the room, the adults murmuring among themselves in a subdued fashion, while the eyes of the Kent children were as wide as saucers, simultaneously thrilled and intimidated by what was taking place. Even Hamlet, evidently aware that something was in the air, lay flat, ears drooping. On the other side of the ballroom, the Polkernow theatre team were seated in a loose group forming something of a protective circle around Matthew Sutcombe, who sat silent and apparently still stunned in their centre.

The inspector stepped up on to the dais at the end of the room. "Thank you for coming," he began, with cursory politeness. "I'm sure you are all aware by now of what has happened. Mr Simeon Ashton-Rose has been found dead, and we are treating the death as suspicious. I shall therefore be interviewing everybody who was present at the village's theatre last night, and for the moment, those premises are off-limits as a potential crime scene."

"Now just a minute, inspector." Leah marched

forward, bristling. "Are you telling us that we may not carry on with our play tonight?"

"That's exactly what I'm saying, madam," replied Tregarth.

After a moment's pause, Leah stepped up alongside the detective and stitched a smile on to her face. "Let me see if I understand you correctly, inspector. Now, I've had a wee word with Tania and Ron here, who were the ones who found the body. And I've no doubt you've examined the place where Simeon was discovered. Am I right?"

"Of course," replied Tregarth uncertainly, clearly unsettled at this line of cross-examination.

"And apart from the late gentleman, there were only two items relating to our play found at the scene, one being the ass's head used during the action, and the other being a bronze feather which functioned as a quill pen. Nothing and nobody else. Correct?"

"That's so," admitted the inspector.

"And I wouldn't mind betting," continued Leah, now well into her stride, "that you've had your forensic people hard at work examining these items, as well as the body. You don't seem to me to be the kind of man who'd let the grass grow under his foot."

Tregarth seemed not to know quite how to interpret this apparent compliment. "Of course. In fact, I'm very proud of the fact that our forensic team are amongst the finest in the land. They've wasted no time in looking at the scene in the minutest detail. In fact, they've worked through the night."

"I'm delighted to hear it," said Leah. Her smile became more wolfish. "So I dare say you're in possession of their findings. They'll have checked our props for fingerprints and done their best to obtain any DNA from them, I'll be bound."

"Naturally, madam," said the inspector. "But you can't expect me to divulge details of any findings to you."

150

"No, of course not, inspector." Leah seemed to be beginning to enjoy herself. "But perhaps I can save you the trouble. Let me tell you what your forensics people will have reported to you. The ass's head will have yielded a mass of fingerprints, most of which will be unidentifiable, but I think I can help you with that. Every member of our theatre company will have, at some time, handled the head. If they haven't worn it during the course of the play's action, they will in all probability have touched it, and quite probably tried it on, during our rehearsals when I was looking the other way, or else been in contact with it when we were setting up here for our performances. And that's not to mention all those people, villagers and tourists, who may well have touched it in passing during yesterday morning's village celebration."

"Celebration? What celebration?" Tregarth, clearly feeling on the back foot, sounded baffled.

Ben Polkerris raised a hand. "It's the Midsummer Mumming, sir. We have an annual parade in the village, and we have the 'Obby Ass, and one of the young chaps here, he had the head on ..."

"All right, all right!" The inspector cut him short. "So, I'm prepared to agree," he continued tight-lipped, "that this donkey's head thing has, according to the SOCO team, been in contact with too many people to yield anything helpful. Although what the dead man was doing apparently wearing it at the time of his death is another question."

"And it's not one you're likely to have answered by keeping us away from the theatre," pounced Leah. "And then, of course, there's that bronze quill. Which you seem to be regarding as a possible murder weapon."

"Of course," grated an irritated Tregarth. "Under the circumstances, I don't see how there can be any doubt."

"You may be right," responded Leah airily. "But I'd just like to ask my friends here." She addressed the group in the ballroom. "Can I have a show of hands? Which of you has handled the quill?" Several hands were raised. "Because Martha here, our Quince, uses it during the action. Our Bottom, Andrew, has a tussle with her over it. Then, of course, it's passed through the hands of several others – probably Reuben Hawke, the stage manager, and Ruth Tresillian, his assistant, who's responsible for laying out the props during the show. And that's not to mention Mary Pengelly, who is in overall charge of props for the theatre, and produced it for us from her stock when our own original feather was damaged. And this quill was, I understand, made for an earlier production here at the theatre, and will have been handled by all manner of previous performers. That will have given your forensics people a right old conundrum, I'm thinking. And no possible way to point a finger at anyone. Any comment, inspector?"

"Your assessment is correct." The admission came through gritted teeth.

"And let me take a wild guess. Your people will have moved on to the backstage area and looked for anything untoward which might account for the presence of Mr Ashton-Rose in this unfortunate situation. You say they're first-class, so I'm sure that if there had been anything worthy of comment, they'd have brought it to your attention. So, was there anything?"

"No," came the curt reply.

"So, to sum up," said Leah, "our props have yielded no helpful evidence, so there is no reason for you to retain the ass's head. Oh, I'm quite happy to let you keep hold of the quill. That was never ours anyway. We can make do. And the *locus in quo* ..." She turned to address the rest of the room. "Sorry; for those not familiar with legal Latin, that means 'the scene of the crime'." She turned back to the inspector. "So, the theatre premises have nothing to tell you. So what possible reason could there be for preventing our continuing with our performances?" she concluded triumphantly.

"Because ... because ..." Tregarth seemed lost for words.

"Er ..." Ben Polkerris spoke up hesitantly. "There'd be another problem if you did cancel them, sir."

"And what might that be, pray?" The inspector's reaction was almost a snarl.

"They've sold out all their performances, sir," said Ben. "We've got hundreds of people coming to the village every night for the rest of the week to see their play. And there's probably no way to get in touch with most of them, what with there being a lot of tourists about the place and all. And I don't know that I'm equipped to handle crowds of annoyed people. It'd be a nightmare. It might do more harm than good if you cancel. And if, as the lady says, there's nothing to find at the theatre ..."

Tregarth stood deep in thought for several long moments, his face like thunder. "Oh, very well," he said eventually. "You can carry on with your blasted play." The beginning of a cheer from the floor was instantly stilled. "Polkerris, I want you there every night. If anything relevant emerges, however small, I want to know immediately. And if this case goes south, somebody's head is going to roll. Sergeant Mitchell!"

"Sir?"

"Take everyone's name and address. I want each of these people interviewed. Organise it!" With a final glare in Leah's direction, Tregarth marched from the room and the door slammed behind him.

There was a collective sigh of relief, as Leah turned to face the company. "Well, ladies and gentlemen, you heard the inspector. Tonight's performance will proceed according to schedule. You will present yourselves on stage five minutes before the half-hour call." She approached Sergeant Mitchell. "You know how to reach me, sergeant. And Reuben, perhaps you'd like to be the first to give the sergeant your details. Because then you and I can go down to the theatre and make sure that Mr Tregarth's minions haven't wrought too much mayhem."

As Mitchell watched Leah and Reuben leave the ballroom, he turned to Tania who was standing nearby. "That," he said, with a rueful smile, "is one pretty tough lady. I've never seen anyone get the better of the guv'nor like that before. I mean, who on earth is she?"

"Leah?" replied Tania airily. "Oh, at home she's just an alpaca farmer."

"A farmer?" The sergeant was disbelieving. "She's not like any of the farmers round here."

"Oh, that's just what she does now," put in Ron. "She used to have another job."

"Oh yes?"

"That's right," said Tania with an impish smile. "Before she gave it up, she used to be a barrister. One of the best, they say. Someone once told me that, around the courts, they used to call her 'the attack dog'. Your boss didn't stand a chance."

*

The members of the play cast gravitated instantly around Tania and Ron as soon as the police presence had absented itself from the ballroom. Sergeant Mitchell, his notebook filled with contact details, had cast one final look of surmise around the room before disappearing in the footsteps of his superior, while Ben Polkerris, deep in hushed conversation with his wife, had led the exodus of the Polkernow residents, with the rest trailing uncertainly behind him.

"So what happened?" eagerly demanded Paul. "Finding a dead body in the middle of the night? That must have been pretty exciting."

"Not as exciting as all that," responded Ron wryly. "We were afraid for a minute that it might be you."

"Me?" The remark had swiftly taken the wind out of Paul's sails. "Why on earth would it be me?"

Tania explained the series of events that had led up to the discovery of the body, and was greeted with a mixture of astonishment and horror. A chorus of questions followed.

"Why was Simeon down in the theatre at that hour?" wondered Timothy.

"And where was Matthew during all this?" enquired Peter.

"Weren't you scared, Tania?" quavered Sarah. "I know I would be." She clutched on to Esther as if for support.

"What was the chap doing mucking about with my ass's head anyway?" asked Andrew sternly. "Surely any theatre person with half a brain knows you don't go messing with other people's props."

"And there was my quill too, don't forget," added Martha, looking slightly queasy. "I'm going to feel really ill during that scene when I use it, even if they find me another one. Is the inspector really sure that it was the murder weapon?"

"Is the inspector really sure that it's a murder?" queried Elizabeth.

"That's right," David joined in, casting a protective eye over the couple's children, who were clustered around him open-mouthed, rapt at all the speculation. "I mean, couldn't Simeon somehow have tripped and fallen on the quill himself? Couldn't the whole thing have been some sort of stupid joke that went wrong?"

"That man didn't seem to be the sort to joke," muttered Susannah. "And he certainly didn't like Hamlet." At the mention of his name, the dog sat up, ears pricked. "I don't think he was very nice."

"That means there's a killer on the loose," declared James with a ghoulish grin. "A homicidal maniac!" He gave his cousin an excited nudge. "Hey, Tom. We could have a go at tracking them down. That'd be something to tell the guys back home. I'm up for that."

"You speak for yourself," riposted Thomas. "If there's some loony going about murdering people, I'm keeping well away."

"We're all keeping well away," intervened David firmly. "Especially you two. I'm in charge of keeping an eye on you, and I'm not going to have you running into any kind of danger. I think the best thing would be for all of us to stick together."

"He's right," said Ron. "Because surely there's no way the police could think that any of us could be involved in this. I mean, we hardly knew the man, and besides, we were all together at the party until just before Tania and I went down to the theatre."

"But that means ..." said Esther, and then stopped short, eyes wide.

"Exactly," said Ron. "Unless James' theory of a homicidal maniac is true, which I have to say is unlikely, then one of the theatre people from the village must have been responsible. Somebody we know. And the question then is, who?"

Chapter 15
Thursday

"I don't know how the police are going to sort all this out," remarked Ron, as he and Tania sat once more on the clifftop bench from which they had first surveyed the panorama of Polkernow Bay. Below them, a pair of choughs wheeled in the crystal-clear air.

"You may have a point," agreed his wife. "They don't seem so far to have much of a clue. Or in fact any clues, from what Inspector Tregarth was saying. Do you suppose that was why he was so cross?"

"I've got a feeling that being cross is probably his default setting," grinned Ron. "And I don't think his little chat with Leah made him feel any happier. But no, being clueless is likely to drive any detective mad."

"Best not call him clueless to his face," smiled Tania. "I don't think it would do much good for his blood pressure."

"No, but it's true," mused Ron. "I mean, there are only a few basic facts. Simeon was out there in his pyjamas in the middle of the night, but we have no idea why. Nor do we know what he was up to with the ass's head, or the quill. If there's no forensics to go on, which Leah more or less forced the inspector to admit, then what's left?"

"I suppose," said Tania slowly, "that there's no mileage in David's suggestion that the whole thing might have been some daft joke that went wrong?"

Ron gave her a look. "I think we know better than that. I reckon David was just clutching at straws so as not to frighten his kids unduly."

"Oh, kids are more robust than that," replied Tania dismissively. "There's nothing they like more than a bit of blood and horror, preferably involving dinosaurs. It's a shame this is Cornwall, and not the Jurassic Coast.

Somebody could have concocted a lovely story for the boys. And didn't some dinosaurs used to have feathers? Could that account for the quill?"

"And before we stray too far into the realms of fantasy," said Ron drily, "we'd probably better stick to the facts. And one of those facts is that Simeon, from all that we knew of him, or have been told about him, wasn't the kind of man to indulge in frivolous japes. It wasn't in his character."

"Ah!" Tania pounced. "That's it. Maybe it's all in his character. Isn't there a saying, 'Know the man and you know his murderer'?"

"Or, if we're being politically correct, 'Know the man, woman, or non-binary individual'?" quipped Ron.

"No, but I'm serious," insisted Tania. "We've been told plenty, from all sorts of people, about how Simeon got on the wrong side of everybody involved with our production at some time or another. So maybe one of these conflicts ran deeper that anyone realises, and that provided enough impetus for somebody to kill him."

"But we also know that, in line with Inspector Tregarth's instructions, the police are going to be interviewing all the people concerned. Surely all this information about what Simeon did to get up such-and-such a person's nose is going to come out."

"I wouldn't bank on it," demurred Tania. "I've got a feeling that, in a place like this, people would be more likely to close ranks and not let the outsiders know all the ins and outs of village life."

"And it's not as if Simeon was the most popular man in the village." Ron shrugged. "Maybe nobody will be too eager to point the finger at one of their friends."

Tania shook her head. "The trouble with that argument is that, if nobody is found to have been responsible, the whole mystery is going to hang over Polkernow like a dark cloud, and people will always be looking sideways at their friends and wondering. No," she stated firmly. "Somebody has to find the answer."

"So, if not the police, who?" Ron chuckled. "You?"

"Is the idea so mad?" bridled Tania.

"No, no, not at all," said Ron hastily. "I mean, you do love a good whodunnit on television, and I bet you've lost count of the number of detective novels you've read, sat behind your counter at work. Handy, being a librarian, isn't it?""

"Exactly! So it's not as if I haven't picked up a thing or two along the way as to how you go about solving a crime."

"For instance?"

"For instance, clever clogs, I know that the police look for the three main factors in a murder. They look at the means, they consider the motive, and they investigate the opportunity. So," said Tania, warming to her theme, "the means. That's obvious. Simeon was stabbed with the bronze quill. Although I haven't quite worked out how Bottom's ass's head fits into the scene, but we'll come to that later. Then, as to motive, we've probably got a sackful. All we have to do is cast our minds back over everything that we've been told, and we can come up with a list."

"And that list is going to have everyone on it," pointed out Ron.

"Some more likely than others." Tania was not to be daunted. "We ought to be able to weed some of them out. But, and here's where you and I have the advantage over the cheery Mr Tregarth, we then come on to the question of opportunity. If the person responsible is one of the theatre personnel, which seems the most likely, then they were all at the after-show party at the pub. And if Simeon was the first to leave, which I seem to remember he was, and you and I were the last, then somewhere in between is the murderer." She gave a little shudder. "I think that's the first time I've used the word. I don't much like the sound of it."

"But you're absolutely right about everything you've said," remarked Ron, impressed. "All you need to do, madam detective, is come up with some answers. And only a couple of days to do it."

*

Ron and Tania approached the White House, surprised to find that there was already a queue of theatre patrons strung out along the lane, several of whom whispered excitedly and gave knowing nods at the couple as they passed.

"Seems as if we've already achieved some sort of notoriety," murmured Ron. "I don't much fancy pushing my way through that lot to get to the front door."

"And it looks as if it's still locked anyway," said Tania. "I doubt if they open it until the half. Let's go round to the side."

At the side gate, they found Luke Crowan, standing sentinel to ensure that only authorised people gained access to the theatre. "Hello," he greeted them, with a slightly wan smile. "Well, that's everyone in now. I'd better get back inside and make sure that we're all ready for me to open the doors."

"How is everyone?" enquired Tania.

"We're all still in something of a state of shock," said Luke. "But everyone's pulling together. Like the old cliché says, the show must go on."

"It looks as if the news about Simeon hasn't put the punters off," remarked Ron. "That's quite a queue you've got out front."

"Yes," agreed Luke ruefully. "Nothing like a scandal to pull the public in. In a way, it's a shame we're already sold out. The news would have got people clamouring to buy tickets." He grimaced. "Which isn't a very tasteful thing to say, but it's true. But at least the fact that we don't have to open the box office means that Matthew doesn't have to worry about that."

"How's he doing?" asked Tania. "Have you seen him?"

"Other than at that session this morning? Yes. I didn't really get the chance to speak to him then, but I popped up to the pub later on and saw him. He's bearing up. And at least he's got Bianca to keep him company."

"Bianca? Who's she?" wondered Ron.

"His dog," explained Luke. "Last seen being fed morsels of chicken fillet by a cooing Angela Hayle."

"Thank goodness for that," said Ron in relief. "For one ghastly moment I was afraid that there was some sort of dreadful love triangle going on. I think Inspector Tregarth would have found that a very interesting potential motive."

Luke gave a dry smile. "Not a particularly likely scenario," he said. "For all Simeon's faults, Matt has always been very loyal to him."

"What, even after that ... incident just before we opened?" queried Tania hesitantly.

Luke shrugged. "Who knows what goes on in a relationship?" He looked at his watch. "Anyway, I'd better get inside. I have to open the doors in five minutes."

"Oh lord," said Ron. "We'd better scoot down or we'll be late for Leah's pep talk, or whatever."

"Break a leg," called Luke, as the pair scuttled round to the terrace and began the descent to the stage.

"I'll keep this brief," said Leah, standing and moving to the centre of the stage as Ron and Tania settled into the front rows of audience seating to join their fellow cast-members, together with Reuben and his backstage crew. "We've all had something of an unpleasant surprise, to put it mildly. This business with Simeon is bound to have unsettled us all." Her voice grew firm. "But that doesn't mean that our audience will

161

expect anything less than our best from all of us. They've come to watch a play, not a car crash. So I want concentration and commitment from everyone. We have a magnificent production. Let's show people just how good the Ramston Operatic And Dramatic Society can be!" Nods and murmurs of agreement all round, and a small ripple of applause. "Well, don't just sit there! Get yourselves ready!" With only a moment's hesitation, the company hurriedly dispersed, as a bell rang from the White House above to signal the arrival of the audience.

*

"We always seem to be last," said Tania as she and Ron emerged from the dressing room corridor on to the stage at the end of the play, to find the theatre deserted with the exception of Reuben Hawke, who stood in the middle of the playing area as if surveying that all in his domain was ready for the next performance.

"You're not wrong," replied Reuben. "Everybody's made their escape, except for you two." He grimaced. "That sounds wrong. I didn't mean ... you know."

"We know what you mean," said Ron.

The stage manager achieved a smile. "Anyway, it all seemed to go well tonight. The audience were saying some pretty good things when I popped out front during the interval, and the applause at the end seemed very generous. So it doesn't look as if the punters have been put off by ..." He sighed. "By Simeon's death. You know, it still seems weird to say it."

"I think we're all trying to get over the weird at the moment," sympathised Tania. "Actually, I felt pretty odd myself when I was doing the scene with Andrew when Bottom had been changed into an ass. I mean, looking into the animal's eyes, saying all the sloppy loved-up lines, I couldn't stop myself thinking about where the ass's head had been less than twenty-four hours before. And earlier I'd happened to peep through to catch a glimpse of Martha when she was doing the business with the quill, and I could see her hand shaking."

"They didn't make her use the bronze one that was stuck in ...?" Ron pulled a face and didn't complete the sentence. "She did say she wasn't looking forward to that bit."

"Oh no," said Reuben hastily. "No, the police have still got that. But that couple of young chaps in your cast – cousins, aren't they? - they went down to the harbour and scrounged up a big seagull wing feather for her to use."

"But we all got through it," said Tania brightly, sounding determined not to be unsettled by the events of the previous night. "How are your team getting on?"

Reuben sighed again. "Well, you can imagine. Everyone's thrown a bit. Not that Simeon ever had anything to do with the actual running of performances, of course, but it's never going to be far from anyone's mind. Everyone seems to be dealing with it in a different way. Judith's worried that everybody is going to be looking at her a bit askance because her husband is part of the police, so they'd be nervous about saying something amiss in front of her. And Mary's jumpy because that prop of hers was found with the body, so she's afraid that the police might think she's tangled up in it somehow. Ruth's worried for Matt, of course, not to mention that dog of his. She's got an even softer spot for Bianca, so she's always bringing her bits of treat from her uncle's shop. And Naomi seems to have just decided to put her shoulders back and concentrate on doing the best job she can, despite what might have been said about her in the past."

"We had a chat with Luke Crowan on our way in tonight," said Ron. "He said much the same thing about people being knocked sideways. And I suppose it's that bit worse for all of you, because you've got the police coming round asking questions."

"That sergeant chap came round to the shop to talk to me today," said Reuben. "Seems we're all suspects. The local theatre team, that is. From what he was saying, I gather that his boss has pretty much ruled out any of you Ramston people. Reckons there's no logical reason for thinking one of your lot could be responsible, so the inspector sent him out to begin quizzing us, starting with me. Not that I was able to tell him much. He wanted to know if Simeon had any enemies."

"What did you say?" enquired Tania.

Reuben gave her a look. "I told him that I couldn't think of anyone who would want to kill him," he said firmly. "Which I reckon was as much as the police needed to know about our business. And he was also asking about people's movements after your first night party."

"And what did you tell him?"

"Not a lot I could tell him," responded the stage manager. "Mainly because I reckon I was probably the first of our crowd to leave. Apart from Simeon and Matt, of course. Simeon's not what you'd describe as a party person at the best of times, and this certainly wasn't that as far as he was concerned, what with one thing and another. But I was pretty worn out – first nights are always tiring because I've got so many things on my mind, always checking that everyone is on top of their job and watching out for anything that could be done better. So I baled out and went home." He smiled grimly. "Which, once I've managed to throw you two out, I intend to do now. Second nights aren't that much easier, you know."

"And we're holding you up. Sorry," said Tania with an apologetic smile. "We're off. Come on, Ron. And we'll see you tomorrow, Reuben." She took her husband's hand, and the two climbed the steps to the top of the auditorium towards the darkened White House. As they passed through the side gate and into the lane, there was a muted 'clunk' as the theatre's working lights were switched off, plunging the establishment into a deep velvet darkness, leavened only by the calm moonlight.

*

"It looks as if what I said was right," said Tania, as the pair made their way up through the silent village towards Hollyhock Cottage. "Sergeant Mitchell is starting to ask questions about what time people left the after-show party. That seems to be what he's concentrating on."

"It'll have to be," agreed Ron. "That's if everyone is as tight-lipped about their various grievances with Simeon as Reuben was just now."

"They may not want to reveal their own problems with him," pointed out Tania, "but there's always the possibility that some inconvenient facts about somebody else might slip out during these interviews. Especially if it's Inspector Tregarth doing the questioning, rather than the considerably more fluffy Sergeant Mitchell."

"And it's not as if we had to crowbar information out of everyone," said Ron. "The gossip just trickled out of its own accord. And Ben Polkerris must know quite a bit of it. The question is, how much is he going to feel bound to pass on to his superiors?"

"That's Mr Tregarth's problem," said Tania. "We've got the advantage over him in that respect. But if we go back to what I was just saying, if we go around having a few more friendly chats, not just with the villagers but with our lot, we might be able to tease out the question of opportunity by working out what sequence everybody left the pub last night. Put that together with motives, and you get ..."

"Bibbidy-bobbidy-boo?" suggested Ron with a grin. "Well, Madam Detective, I shall enjoy watching you do your stuff."

"Oh no," retorted Tania. "I'm not doing all the heavy lifting. You're helping."

"Right, ma'am," said Ron, sketching a mock salute. "Just one question."

"What's that?"

"Which one shall I be – Doctor Watson or Captain Hastings?"

Chapter 16
Friday

"How are you going to tackle this?" wondered Ron, as he finished putting the breakfast things away. "I mean, aren't people going to find it a bit strange if you start going around cross-examining them? They're going to wonder what you're up to."

"I can be subtle," replied Tania.

"You're going to have to manufacture reasons to seek out people," pointed out Ron. "It's not as if we can wait until we're at the theatre this evening and then line everyone up and quiz them."

"I haven't the slightest intention of doing anything of the kind," retorted his wife.

"Thank goodness for that," grinned Ron. "I had some horrible image of you standing there, surrounded by suspects, expounding your theories as arrived at by the exercise of your little grey cells, until at the end you pointed a dramatic finger and announced 'So it was you!'."

"Idiot!" laughed Tania. "No, we shall do exactly what we did when we first got here, which is stroll idly around the village, just as if we were on holiday, and fall into casual conversation with whoever we chance to meet. It's a beautiful day again, so why wouldn't we? So I suggest you stop swanning around in that dressing-gown like the Sheikh of Araby, go and put some touristy clothes on, and we shall commence our wander."

"Your wish is my command, O She Who Must Be Obeyed," replied her husband with a bow, just avoiding the flying tea-cosy which followed him out of the door.

Some few minutes later, the couple were on their way hand-in-hand down Fore Street, following Tania's suggestion that they could easily begin by dropping in to the 'A Cake and a Cuppa' cafe for elevens, when their attention was attracted by the sound of a bump, followed by muttered curses, coming from the other side of the garden wall of one of the cottages they were passing.

A hand clad in a gardening glove appeared on the crest of the wall, followed by the slightly dirt-smudged face and overall-clad form of Naomi Constantine as she heaved herself to her feet. "Sorry," she smiled. "Hope I didn't make you jump."

"Not at all," replied Tania.

"Only it's this blasted ground elder," continued Naomi, holding aloft a tussock of some indeterminate white-flowered foliage. "I foolishly offered to do some gardening for my parents, because they're both finding it a bit of a challenge, what with my dad's back and my mother's eyesight not being what it used to be. And Luke was supposed to be helping me, but he's cleverly managed to go missing, so I thought I'd make a start on it myself. And let me tell you," she said, "it's damned hot work in this weather." She scrubbed ineffectually at her face with the back of her hand.

"You look as if you could do with a break," observed Ron. "As one of nature's great non-gardeners, you have my sympathy."

"Speaking of sympathy," said Tania, "how is everybody coping with all this Simeon business? I wondered, because I haven't really had a chance to chat with anyone about it. I mean, it's not exactly easy for us in the play cast who hardly knew him, but it must be awful for those of you who were more involved with the running of the theatre."

Naomi perched on the wall, a look of consideration on her face. "The policeman said something of the sort to me yesterday. Oh, not that inspector chap. I don't think he does sympathy, but I suppose in his position, you wouldn't. But the sergeant who came to talk to me – Mitchell, isn't it? - he was nicer. Wanted to know if anyone might have had anything against Simeon which could have led to them wanting to harm him."

"And I suppose you probably couldn't offhand think of anything?" enquired Tania blandly.

"Not why someone would kill him," said Naomi swiftly.

"Why can't people concentrate on the happier times?" jumped in Ron. "I mean, the last time we all saw Simeon was at the after-show party, wasn't it? I think I prefer to remember everyone enjoying themselves."

Naomi raised an eyebrow. "I'm not sure you'd exactly say Simeon was having a good time at your party. In fact, he looked pretty sour, from what I remember. And I know he left quite early. Even before us, and we didn't exactly stay late."

"Us?" queried Tania.

"Luke and me. I remember, we were wondering how soon we could decently get away – oh, nothing to do with the party," added Naomi hastily. "No, that was good fun, and you were all celebrating because of how well the show had gone. But I noticed Reuben made his excuses to Leah and left, and I thought we could take that as our cue to slide out as well. I had a couple of music cues that I wanted to check on on my master disc, because they hadn't gone exactly right during the performance."

"I didn't notice anything wrong," said Ron.

"You probably wouldn't," smiled Naomi. "But I did. I wanted everything to be spot on. I'm a bit of a perfectionist like that, despite ... well, despite one or two comments I've had in the past. So Luke walked me home, and then I came in and went through the music, and then went to bed."

"Was there anybody about around the village at that time?" wondered Tania.

"No, not a soul. Reuben had already vanished, and the audience were long gone, so everything was quiet.

And my parents were long in bed and asleep by then. But then, of course, next morning ... well, you know what we all woke up to."

"We do," nodded Ron. "Anyway, we mustn't keep you from your gardening. I'm sure you're eager to get back to it."

"Thanks for the reminder," grunted Naomi. "Oh well, no rest for the wicked. But I'll be having a few words with Luke when he turns up." She hopped down from the wall and, with a sigh, got back on her hands and knees.

*

"Now that may be instructive," observed Tania as she and Ron continued down Fore Street towards the village centre.

"How do you mean?"

"Didn't you notice? Naomi told us Luke walked her home, but she said that 'I' came in to work on the sound. Alone. So where did Luke go? And if she was on her own, that means that she can't provide an alibi for the relevant time."

"Either for herself, or for him."

"Wonder what he'll have to say for himself. Well, that's one for the back burner for now," said Ron "In the meantime, we have other fish to fry. Or cakes to consume," he added, as he pushed open the door of 'A Cake and a Cuppa' and ushered his wife inside.

"Hello, my loves." Judith Polkerris greeted the couple with a smile which contained only the slightest traces of strain. "Nice to see you. What can I get you?"

"We thought we'd treat ourselves to a cake and a cuppa," smiled Ron, "since that's obviously what you do best."

"Well, it's a treat to have you say so," said Judith. "And it makes a change to have somebody in here this morning."

Tania surveyed the empty tables in the establishment. "It doesn't look as if you're exactly run off your feet at the moment," she observed sympathetically.

"Hardly," replied Judith. "One table I've had so far this morning, and that was just the chap delivering some paint for Reuben's shop who wanted a quick coffee and the loo. I don't know where people are."

"The village did seem a bit quiet as we were walking down," said Ron. "I should have thought the place would be swarming at this time of year. But it's still fairly early in the day for the tourists. I expect it'll get busier later."

"I hope you're right," replied Judith gloomily. "I just hope people aren't staying away because of ... well, you know."

"Oh, surely not," said Tania brightly. "In fact, I'd have thought a touch of notoriety might have brought the rubberneckers flocking. You know what people are like."

"But I can see that the whole Simeon situation must have cast something of a pall," said Ron. "We were just chatting with Naomi, and she said she felt it was just a question of getting on with it and trying not to think too much about things."

"And in that spirit," intervened Tania with determination, "we'll have a pot of tea for two, and a couple of slices of that wonderful chocolate gateau of yours."

"Right you are. Now, why don't you have a seat at that nice table in the front window where you can see what's going on in the street. And you never know, you might even attract me some customers. Back in a jiff." Judith disappeared in the direction of the kitchen.

A few minutes later, as Judith deposited the tea things and the two plates of cake in front of her customers, Tania resumed the conversation. "Anyway, how are you getting on yourself? We haven't really had a chance to speak since Wednesday night, have we? I mean, it's all very well for Naomi to talk about trying to forget about the situation, but it must be that much more difficult for you, what with your husband being involved in the investigation. But I suppose he can't talk about it."

"Well, he's certainly not supposed to." Judith gave a slightly evasive wriggle. "But that Sergeant Mitchell, he came round asking questions, wanting to know all about Simeon and how he got on with people in the village, but I told him that we aren't the sort of people to go gossiping about our neighbours, and I left it at that. But I don't think he was too happy with what I'd said, and he said he'd probably get better information out of a trained officer like my Ben."

"Did you forget to tell him about that little matter between you and Simeon?" enquired Tania innocently. "Don't I remember Matthew mentioning some dispute between you and Simeon over the running of the cafe at the theatre?"

"Oh, that. That was just a storm in a teacup," said Judith. She gave an exaggeratedly carefree laugh. "Here, hark at me. Teacup! That was very funny, wasn't it?" Her face sobered. "But no, that was just a misunderstanding. It was straightened out quite easily. So I really didn't think that Sergeant Mitchell needed to know about it." She paused, and a slight look of worry came over her features. "But maybe I should have said something, or else he might get the wrong end of the stick. I mean, Ben might mention it in passing."

"You mean when he was telling his superiors about his own little spats with Simeon?" suggested Ron guilelessly. "After all, if Simeon had made complaints about Ben, that could well have reached the ears of someone like Inspector Tregarth."

"Oh, I'm sure there's nothing to worry about," soothed Tania. "Anyway, let's not talk about the inspector. He's enough to put a dampener on anything." She took a fork-full of gateau. "Maybe you should feed him some of this delicious cake. That'd sweeten him up."

"It's very kind of you to say so," said Judith with a brave smile.

"And it's just as good as I remember," put in Ron. "Didn't we have some of this at our after-show party?"

"That's right. In fact, I brought one along because I knew people might fancy something a bit sweet, what with all the savoury snacks and what-have-you, and it ended up with the whole thing being demolished. So I thought I'd better come and make another couple, else I'd have had none for when I opened up in the morning."

"What, you came back here and started baking after the party?" Tania's attention was alerted.

"Oh, I quite often do something last thing at night," said Judith. "It gives the cakes a chance to cool down overnight so that I can get on with the decoration first thing. Baking's my relaxation. It helps me settle. So I came away and got started on a fresh couple of cakes."

"And I never got the chance to thank you for your contribution to the party," apologised Tania. "I suppose all of us in the cast were too much tied up with one another to notice you go. So what time would that have been, do you think?"

"Oh, I couldn't say. Not that early, and most of our people had already gone. Although our Mary was still there when I came away. She might remember. Actually, she was probably the last of our lot, but I suppose she would be, being as how she works for Toby, so I expect she felt an obligation to help with the clearing-up. I remember Simeon and Matthew went quite early on, but I'm not sure about the others. But I suppose they must have left before me, so they might know times. Why, is it important?"

"Oh no, not in the least," Tania reassured her.

"Maybe Ben would know."

"No, he wouldn't. After all, it's not as if we live here at the cafe, and anyway, he always goes for a late-night stroll round the village, just to check up on things. Normally he pops down to the harbour, because there's quite often a bit of a kerfuffle with one or two of the lads who've been drinking down there. So I didn't see him at all that night."

"What, not even when Tania came up to fetch him down to the theatre?" wondered Ron.

"No," replied Judith. "I think I must have been dead to the world by then."

"Oh?" Tania raised an eyebrow.

"Yes," said Judith. "I'd got one of my headaches while I was cooking," she explained ruefully. "Come on something terrible, they do. Black and white zigzags, I get. And I was just putting the cakes in the oven, but by then I could hardly see, so I phoned the pub and got our Mary to come down and finish off for me, and I went home and took a couple of my knockout pills. Didn't know a thing until next morning."

"So you can't ...?"

Before Tania could complete her question, the bell over the cafe's front door jingled into life, and a couple entered, followed by a pair of young children. With an abrupt reversion to her customary bonhomie, Judith turned to them with a welcoming smile. "Good morning, my loves," she greeted them. "What can I get you?"

"Are we too early for one of your cream teas?" ventured the wife. "Only we've been reading your sign ..."

"Never too early in the day for a cream tea, my dear," trilled Judith. "And I think you'll find we've got just the thing. Especially for these two youngsters of yours. So you just sit yourselves down – that table in the corner there's probably best - and I'll be there with our menu in two ticks." She turned back to Ron and Tania and lowered her voice. "Well, I must get on. But it's been lovely chatting to you." Casting a slightly forced smile behind her, she bustled away to the counter.

*

"So, Miss Marple, was that at all helpful, do you think?" enquired Ron, after he and Tania had finished their elevenses, settled their bill, and emerged once more on to Fore Street.

"Difficult to tell," said Tania. "I suppose the only thing it tells us is that it doesn't tell us very much."

"Oh, extremely helpful," grinned Ron. "I don't know how you do it."

"No, what I mean is," replied Tania, her brow furrowed in thought, "is that, for a start, we can't be sure yet as to the sequence of people leaving the party."

"Oh, I don't know. Surely we can work it out. If Simeon and Matthew left first, and then Reuben was the next to go, that narrows it down. And if Judith says that Mary was left as the only one of the theatre crew after she went back to her shop to do her baking, that means that Luke and Naomi came after Reuben, with Ruth somewhere in the middle. I reckon that's as close as we can get without lining them all up."

Tania considered for a moment. "Okay, that's fair enough. But what we also now have is a very unhelpful absence of alibi for the two sisters. How convenient was that headache of Judith's, I wonder? I mean, she could have manufactured it if she had in mind to go down to the theatre and have some sort of confrontation with Simeon, even though that may sound pretty far-fetched. So, whether what she told us is true or not, she called her sister in and left her alone in the shop, baking. But what about when the cakes came out of the oven? There's Mary, on her own, with nobody to vouch for her. And she's got plenty of reasons to dislike Simeon."

"Something else that struck me," remarked Ron,

175

"was when Judith was talking about Ben. She was pretty evasive when she said that he's not supposed to talk about the case. I'm sure that's true in theory, but if you and I were in the same position, I bet I wouldn't be able to resist dropping a few juicy snippets about how things were going. So I bet she knows more than she's letting on."

"Of course, without meaning to, she's also dropped her own husband in it," observed Tania. "Because if he wasn't around when she got home with this famous headache, then not only can't he vouch for her, but she can't vouch for him. He'd not had the chummiest of relationships with Simeon, by all accounts. So he may well have been off prowling around the village, but we don't know where this prowl took him."

"You know, all this talk about headaches is starting to give me one of my own," confessed Ron. "Can I make a suggestion?"

"Of course."

"Let's pack in the pate-cudgelling for the day. You did say earlier that we should do some touristy wandering, so why don't we give our brains a rest and do just that? I for one could fancy another stroll down to the harbour. You never know – once we've had a bit of a walk, we might be up for one of those crab sandwiches the place down there was advertising. 'Nippers', wasn't it?"

"I believe you're right." Tania threaded her arm through Ron's. "So, a stroll it is. And since you paid for the cakes, the sandwiches are on me."

"Deal!" Ron smiled happily, and the two headed for St. Petroc's church and the top of the harbour lane.

Chapter 17
Friday

"Looks as if there's no escape from your sleuthing activities." Ron gave a rueful chuckle and nodded his head in the direction of a solitary disconsolate figure, alone apart from a small white bundle of fluff on the ground alongside him, sitting on a bollard at the extreme seaward end of the harbour wall. "Unless you'd rather not ..."

Tania sighed. "No. We might as well. Strike while the suspect is hot, and all that." She led the way in the direction of the figure and, as she approached, hailed him in cheery tones. "Hello, Matthew."

Matthew Sutcombe turned from gazing out over the sea and slowly focussed on the newly-arrived pair. "Oh, hello, Tania," he said, with a wan smile. "And Ron."

Tania crouched down alongside the young man's companion. "And hello to you too, Bianca." The dog, in a distinct departure from her earlier behaviour, seemed to have caught the subdued mood and, instead of her previous noisy barking, gave a tentative sniff at Tania's hand and submitted to having her ears fondled.

"She seems to have calmed down a bit," observed Ron, perching on an adjacent bollard.

"You're ..." Matthew cleared his throat, which was evidently rusty from lack of recent use. "You're honoured. Usually she barks at everyone. Well, almost everyone. And she's very sensitive to atmosphere. She doesn't like being away from home."

"You're still at the pub, then?" enquired Tania. "Won't the police let you go back into the White House?"

"Oh, they've said I can," said Matthew, "but ... well, you know."

"It would be uncomfortable, to say the least," sympathised Tania. "I understand that. Although at least, if you were back there running the theatre box office, it would give you something to occupy you. It might take your mind off ... things," she finished, rather lamely.

"Except, of course, that the tickets for the show are all sold out," pointed out Ron. "So I suppose you must be at a bit of a loose end."

Matthew sighed and nodded. "I don't really know what to do with myself. I mean, Toby and Angela have been very kind, and they've said I can stay as long as I like at the pub, but I feel awkward. And there isn't any contribution I can make at the theatre. And even if I did go back, it would be the same as where I am now. Everybody walking on eggshells." He gave a small humourless laugh. "All except the police, of course."

"You said they'd spoken to you," said Tania. "Does that mean they've actually interviewed you about Wednesday night?"

"Yes."

"Not that Inspector Tregarth, I hope. I can't imagine him walking on eggshells," huffed Tania.

"He was there," replied Matthew. "Looming in the background like some figure of doom. But it was Sergeant Mitchell who did most of the talking."

"Thank goodness for that!"

"And he wanted to know what happened on Wednesday, right from the start of the evening, so of course I told him."

"You mean from the time when everybody gathered at the theatre before the performance?"

"That's right. He wanted to know where Simeon was, who he talked to and where he went. And so, because we were together for most of the time, I was able to tell him."

"Including that ..." Tania shifted in embarrassment. " ... that moment in the White House cafe before the show."

178

Matthew reddened slightly. "I said we'd had words. I didn't go into chapter and verse. And I heard the inspector mutter something about 'a lovers' tiff' in the background, but I ignored him."

"Where were you during the play?" wondered Ron.

"Sat right at the back," replied Matthew. "There's a pair of house seats in the back row that we never sell, so we sat there. They're next to each other, of course, so we weren't exactly comfortable."

"That's what you get with concrete seats," quipped Ron, immediately regretting his flippancy.

"No, I mean because of the atmosphere," continued Matt. "But I tried to concentrate on enjoying the play. And it's not as if it's the first time Simeon and I had had an argument, and I've always done my best to get past it before."

"And of course, you were at our after-show party following the performance," resumed Tania. "I remember, you and I had that lovely talk at the Feast, but we never got to speak at the party. Because the two of you left quite early, didn't you?"

"Simeon wanted to go home. He said he wasn't really in the mood for partying, so we came away. And when we got home ... well, of course, the one who was happiest about that was Bianca. Weren't you, baby?" Matthew bent down and ruffled the dog's head. "She made a real fuss of me, jumping and barking as if I'd been away for months, but unfortunately that didn't go down well with Simeon, so I decided that if he was going to be that grumpy, I'd just sleep in the spare room that night to give him a chance to get over it. So we went in there, didn't we, Bianca? You came up and slept on the bed, and I put my earplugs in, and we both settled down for a lovely night's sleep. Until ..."

"Until we appeared with the police." Ron completed the sentence. "And you hadn't heard anything

179

before that?"

"Not a thing. I wouldn't, with the earplugs. But I'm sure that Bianca would have barked if there had been anything unusual happening. She's got amazing hearing." He gave a wan smile. "That used to cause trouble whenever there was a performance at the theatre, until I had the idea of making a little snug for her in the old pantry, and leaving some music on so she couldn't hear what was going on elsewhere."

"Do you have any idea why Simeon would have gone outside after going to bed?" enquired Tania. "Because he was wearing pyjamas, wasn't he?"

"The police asked me that," replied Matthew. "I told them I didn't have a clue. And they asked me about the ass's head and the quill, and whether I could account for them being at the scene, but I told them I was just as puzzled as they were. And they wanted to know whether Simeon had any enemies, and I almost felt like laughing, for all that it wasn't even remotely funny. The words sounded so melodramatic. And I thought, where do I start? I'm not blind. I've seen what's gone on. The village is full of people who disliked Simeon, some more, some less. But enemies?" The young man sounded incredulous. "Someone who hated him enough to kill him?" Matthew shook his head. "It all seemed so far-fetched."

*

"It doesn't sound as if the police went quite as far as accusing Matthew," observed Ron as the couple, having gently extracted themselves from the conversation and left Matthew to resume his unfocused survey of the sea, headed back along the harbour wall. "But I bet that's got to be one of the things they're considering."

"It's bound to be," agreed Tania. "If everyone else has been as cagey talking to the police as it sounds, then Matthew is the only one with a sniff of a motive - that's if

Inspector Tregarth's remark about a 'lovers' tiff' means that he's taking it seriously. And you must admit, it was quite a moment when Simeon delivered that slap. It certainly stopped the rest of us short when it happened."

"And Matthew was the only one who was on the spot at the theatre at the time," said Ron. "Although having said that, we can't be sure that nobody else could have been, what with this constant procession of non-alibis we've heard about. So, since we're absolutely no further forward in your sleuthing efforts, there is in my opinion only one thing left to do."

"And what's that?"

"Eat," grinned Ron. "I seem to remember someone promising to treat me to a crab sandwich. And I'm sure Napoleon must have said something about a detective force marching on its stomach."

His wife grimaced. "And with that elegant image in mind, I think we'd better head for 'Nipper's Nook'."

Tania and Ron weren't the only ones with the same idea, and as they approached the cafe they could see that the area of tables set out at the front on the quayside was packed with holidaymakers, while a glance through the windows showed that the interior appeared to be bulging at the seams. However, the pair were lucky. Just as they reached the establishment, a couple rose from a tiny table tucked into a corner of the terrace, and Ron darted forward to claim a place before any of the other hovering tourists could occupy it. As they sat, they were submerged in the cheerful hubbub, as the young waiting staff, clad in distinctive blue-and-white striped tops and red neckerchiefs, executed a constant complicated interweaving ballet as they squeezed between tables to deliver orders of food and drinks to eager chattering customers. With the cafe this busy, the pair were resigned to a probable long wait before anyone even registered their presence, let alone came to take their order, so they were pleasantly surprised when, after only a couple of minutes spent perusing the menu, a young woman almost skidded to a halt at their table and enquired, in an unexpected Eastern European accent, "What would you like, my loves?"

Ron couldn't stop himself chuckling. "Now that," he laughed, "is the sort of Cornish welcome we've come to expect, but I hope you're not going to try to tell us that you come from round here."

The waitress laughed in return. "You are right, sir. I'm from Estonia. But the boss here, he likes us to do things the proper local way. He says it is friendlier."

"And so it is," smiled Tania. "And we would like two of your De-luxe Crab Sandwich Specials, please, with the salad on the side, and two glasses of cider."

"The House Scrumpy? It is the most popular."

"Why not?"

"Right-oh, my loves," responded the waitress in her finest Baltic Cornish accent, and scooted away, leaving Ron and Tania submerged in a fit of the giggles.

Some time later, Ron leaned back in his chair with a satisfied sigh. "That, my darling, was the finest crab sandwich ever put on God's earth," he said. "I believe the locals would call it 'a proper job'. You certainly know how to treat a man."

"Are you sure that's not just the cider talking?" queried Tania with a smile. "It's pretty strong stuff."

"So much the better," beamed Ron. "I shall enjoy my siesta even more."

"Then I suppose we'd better make a move," said Tania, "or else you'll be falling asleep in the street. And I'm not carrying you back!" The bill paid, the couple rose and threaded their way between the tables to leave, and were just about to begin their return towards Hollyhock Cottage when they almost collided with a young man emerging from a door squeezed between the cafe and

Madame Demelza's adjacent premises.

"Whoa, sorry!" exclaimed the new arrival.

"Luke!" said Tania in surprise. "Fancy running into you."

"Almost literally," smiled Luke Crowan. "But it's not really that astonishing, since I live here."

"Here?" Tania was taken aback. "I'd got the impression you lived at the White House. I thought, because when we first met you, you were coming out and locking the door ..."

"Ah. Easy mistake to make. And in fact I did live there for a while."

"What, you mean in Simeon's flat?" enquired Ron. "That must have been cosy."

"Hmmm." Luke gave a rueful grin. "Cosy is not exactly the word I'd have used. And anyway, I wasn't staying at the flat itself. No, there's a little apartment over what used to be the garage of the house. More of a bedsit, really. I think it must have been where the chauffeur or the gardener lived when the old ladies first had the house built. And then when the house was converted into its current incarnation after they died, the chauffeur's room was turned into a sort of tied cottage for the front-of-house manager. So that's where I used to lay my head."

"But not any more?" Tania's raised eyebrows invited more explanation.

"No. Things got somewhat awkward. Simeon decided that he had ... certain problems with my presence."

"Would that have been because ..." Tania began, but broke off. "Oh dear. I don't quite know how to put this. You see, we were having a chat with Toby Hayle at the pub ..."

Luke laughed. "And he relayed the gossip about Simeon's lunatic accusations about Matt and me? Is that it?"

Tania pulled a face. "Sorry. I feel awful about listening to gossip. It's not something I normally do." Beside her, Ron seemed to develop a sudden fit of coughing. "And I imagine it's the sort of thing nobody really wants talked about."

Luke gave another carefree laugh. "Oh, it doesn't bother me. The entire thing was so palpably insane. And in fact, don't worry about being discreet, because the whole daft story was all round the village before you could say knife. Of course, everyone discounted it, because they'd all seen Naomi and me together, and they knew me well enough by then to know that I'm not the sort of person to go sneaking around. But the situation up at the White House got very uncomfortable, so I moved out and got this little flat over the shop down here. And the good thing is, Grandy doesn't charge me a bean for it."

"Grandy?"

"Well, she's my great-aunt really, but I've always called her 'Grandy'. It's a sort of mash-up of 'great-aunt' and 'Demelza'."

"Madame Demelza is your great-aunt?" Ron sounded incredulous.

"I don't shout about it," chuckled Luke. "Some people think she's a bit weird. But she's always been very good to me. And in fact, she told me not to fret about this business with Simeon, because it would all blow over. Although ..." Luke's expression became serious. "She did say that there was ill fortune in the future, but that I was in no danger. Which actually came as something of a relief. Job-wise, I mean."

"Oh yes," nodded Tania. "Toby mentioned that Simeon had tried to make trouble for you, but it came to nothing in the end. Although I expect the police must have looked at that with some suspicion when you told them."

"I haven't," said Luke. "Not that I've actually been avoiding them. It's just that they haven't got round to me yet, I suppose. But I'm sure they'll quiz me on my movements on the night in question, and whether I'd seen anyone or anything suspicious, and whether I had any motive to wish Simeon ill. Isn't that the way it always goes in these crime thrillers on TV?"

"So what did you do on Wednesday night?" asked Tania guilelessly. "Because I don't think we got a chance to say goodnight to you after our party."

"Naomi said he walked her home," put in Ron. "Don't you remember, love, she told us that when we saw her earlier."

"Of course. I'd forgotten." Tania flicked a slightly irritated glance at her husband. "And then I suppose you must have come back here, Luke?" she persisted. "So you wouldn't have been anywhere near the White House that night?"

Luke shifted awkwardly. "Actually, I was. It was stupid, really. After I left Naomi, I couldn't for the life of me remember whether I'd locked up the French doors leading out to the terrace at the back. It's normally part of my front-of-house routine, but I couldn't recall doing it, what with all the first night congratulations that were going around – it was like one of those 'did I turn the gas off?' moments - so I decided to check. Of course, I knew Simeon had gone back home quite early on, and I was desperate to avoid him seeing me and thinking I was up to no good, plus I didn't want to set Bianca off by making a noise, so I tiptoed round the side of the house and checked the doors as quietly as I could. And they were all firmly shut, so I crept down to the stage level, nipped up the side lane, and came back home."

"And you saw nobody?"

"Not a soul. The place was as silent as the ... the

proverbial."

"You'll need to tell the police all that when they finally catch up with you," said Ron.

"And I'll tell you someone else who's rather anxious to catch up with you," added Tania, "and that's Naomi. You're not exactly in her best books at the moment."

"How so?" Luke looked puzzled.

"Because when we saw her, she was engaged in some fairly strenuous gardening, which she said you were supposed to be helping her with."

Luke's hand went to his brow. "Oh lord! I'd totally forgotten. I'd better shift." He looked down at the smart shirt and trousers he was wearing. "But not like this. I think I ought to change. So if you don't mind ..." With a look of apology, he thrust his key into the door and vanished inside.

*

"Well, there's one question answered," remarked Ron, as he and Tania climbed back up the lane from the harbour. "Now we know where Luke went after he walked Naomi home after the party."

"We know something else as well," pointed out Tania. "Don't you remember? On Wednesday night, after we'd found Simeon and the police had all arrived, when we went back up to the White House, we found one of the French doors to the terrace unfastened. So if Luke had made sure they were secured, that leaves two options. Either somebody else has a key and re-opened the door from the outside ..."

"... or else it was Simeon himself who opened them from the inside," concluded Ron. "Which seems most plausible, considering that he ended up on the outside. But why?"

"And there's another question which occurs to me, and which I should think might equally well occur to the police. We've only got Luke's word for it that he went to the White House to check the security. Could he have gone there for some other reason? Is his version just made up to account for his presence, in case he was seen by somebody?"

"Surely you're not thinking there's some substance to this accusation by Simeon about him and Matthew?" enquired Ron.

"No, of course not. I'm discounting that. My gaydar may not be brilliant, but it's good enough for that." Tania sighed in frustration. "In fact, I don't know what to think. And what's baffling me is, what on earth was Simeon doing on stage, stabbed, and wearing the ass's head? We're no nearer figuring that out."

Ron put his arm round his wife's shoulder. "You, my darling, are desperately in need of something to take your mind off the case. And I'm still looking forward to that siesta of mine. And my question is ..." He directed a roguish sideways glance towards Tania. "Am I going to have to siesta alone, or can we take your mind off things together?"

"Mr Faye, you are a very bad man!" Tania gave her husband a playful slap, and the two resumed their laughing walk towards Hollyhock Cottage.

Chapter 18
Saturday

"Is it odd," mused Tania over breakfast, "that last night's performance seemed completely normal?"

"Normal is fine as far as I'm concerned," replied Ron. "The last thing I need is the excitement of somebody forgetting their lines or not coming on at the right moment."

"No, that's not what I meant. It was almost as if Simeon's death hadn't happened. I mean, all the crew went about their normal duties, and there was no sort of atmosphere like the one on Thursday night when everyone was a bit jumpy, and nobody in our team even mentioned Simeon at all. But I just can't stop wondering ..."

Ron smiled at his wife. "You're like a dog with a bone," he said indulgently. "But just think. After tonight's show, we're away from here, and you can relax and leave the whole thing in the hands of the police. They'll sort it out in time. And you'll never have to think about Simeon Ashton-Rose ever again."

"I know." Tania gave a rueful sigh. "It's the not knowing. But don't forget, there are still a couple of people we haven't spoken to. Not that there's been much of an opportunity at the theatre. Ruth Tresillian is always rushing about making sure that the props have been put back in the right place when they come offstage, or else helping to move furniture, and Mary Pengelly is either up in the theatre cafe getting refreshments ready, or serving them, or washing up afterwards, or else she's working a shift at the pub. That's when she's not helping out baking cakes for her sister in the middle of the night."

"And you are determined to track them down today, because you won't rest until you've ticked them off your list, will you?"

"Am I so transparent?"

"Utterly." Ron leaned across to give his wife a kiss. He thought for a moment. "So, here's a plan. I did think that we might walk over to the tin mine museum this morning, just for a change of scenery. You never know, we might manage to work up a bit of an appetite for a cup of tea and a snack at the Piggery. And we could pop into the butcher's shop on the way back to see if we can catch Ruth for a chat."

"Isn't it going to look a bit obvious if we go in there looking for her, and I then start asking questions about Wednesday night?" Tania sounded dubious.

"Not at all," returned Ron. "This is where my cunning plan comes into its own. Don't you remember – when we were talking pasties with Toby Hayle at the pub, he happened to mention that Angela's home-made were, in his opinion, even better than the award-winning ones that they sell in Tresillian's butchers. So your character's motivation, my dear actress, is that we want to take a taste of Cornwall home with us, and a couple of pasties will fit the bill. And a conversation will ensue. Voilà!"

"And then?"

"Well, a snack at the tin mine isn't going to keep us going, is it?" said Ron reasonably. "We're going to need a proper meal to get us through the day. I think a late lunch. And where better than the Pilchard's Arms? Where we're highly likely to encounter Mary, who we know loves to chat."

"You've thought this all through, haven't you?" remarked Tania in admiring tones.

"I have my uses," replied Ron, trying not to sound smug. "Then we'll come back here and pack up our stuff, so that after doing tonight's show and spending however-long-it-takes clearing all the play equipment from the theatre afterwards, we can be off home first thing. I've loved being here, but I'm looking forward to sleeping in my own bed."

"With a mystery unsolved?"

"If that's the way it has to be," said Ron firmly. "But for this morning, we're still on holiday. So get some sunscreen on your nose, and we'll be off."

The bright sunshine, the lively yet warm breeze which bowled along a procession of small fluffy white clouds in an enormous bright blue sky inhabited by flights of screaming swifts, and the generous slice of lardy cake, oozing with syrup, which accompanied a pot of sturdy tea at the Piggery cafe, all conspired to drive away any thoughts of the mystery surrounding the death of Simeon Ashton-Rose until the couple were descending the hill past the caravan site on their way back into the centre of Polkernow. Arriving at the door of Tresillian's Butchers, they exchanged a swift wordless glance, before Ron nodded and pushed open the door for Tania to pass through.

At the sound of the bell above the door, the solitary occupant of the shop gave a cheerily smiling 'Good day to you both!'. He was a rotund little man clad in a blue-and-white striped apron, with a rosy complexion and impressive mutton-chop whiskers, only lacking a straw boater to complete a striking resemblance to the plaster pig figure which adorned his window display, now surrounded by an elaborate arrangement of fanned cutlets and steaks, gaggles of poultry, and festoons of sausages. "How can I help you folks?" he enquired, laying down a fearsome-looking saw with which he had been attacking a rack of ribs.

"Would you be Mr. Tresillian?" enquired Tania.

"The same," replied the shop-owner. "Abel Tresillian, at your service. And what would you be wanting today?"

"Pasties!" leapt in Ron, as Tania seemed to hesitate.

190

"We've heard that you sell very good pasties."

"That we do," nodded the butcher complacently. "Obviously somebody's been singing our praises."

"We were talking to Mr. Hayle at the pub, and he happened to mention that yours were almost as good as his wife's," explained Tania.

Tresillian burst out chuckling. "That Toby! He never misses a chance to enjoy a little game of one-upmanship. Almost, indeed!" He lowered his voice. "Mind you, between you, me, and the gatepost, he might have the rights of it. His Angela does make the finest home-made pasties this side of the Tamar. Now I can't claim as much, being as mine come from a little bakery just over by Truro who make them special for me with my own best meat, but don't you dare let on I said that."

"Your secret is safe with us," smiled Ron. "So anyway, since they come so highly recommended, we thought we'd buy a couple of your pasties to take home with us to remind us of our stay in Cornwall, seeing as we're off in the morning."

"Ah, you'll be with the theatre people then," said Tresillian. "Actually in the play, are you?"

"We are," said Tania. "Actually, we've got the main parts, so it's been quite a busy week for us."

"Oh, then I know who you are," beamed the butcher. "You'll be Mr and Mrs Faye. Our Ruth's mentioned you. She says you're very good. Well, all your lot are, according to her. But we'll find that out for ourselves this evening, I'm sure. My missus and I are coming to see tonight's performance."

"Then I hope you won't be disappointed," said Tania. "Tell me, is Ruth about, by any chance?"

"She isn't," replied Tresillian. "You'd normally always catch her here on a Saturday, but not just now."

"Oh dear. I hope she's alright." Tania was concerned. "Not that I'd be surprised if she was upset by

191

what's gone on this week at the theatre with Mr. Ashton-Rose."

"No, that was a terrible business," nodded Tresillian. "And the police no nearer finding out what happened, from what I hear. But, bless you, no, Ruth is fine. A bit quiet, but that'll be true of most folks, I reckon. And she's working here today as normal, except I sent her on an errand a little while ago. Dear old Mrs Penrose up the village – sweet old soul, she is, getting on for ninety, but as sprightly as you please. Except that she had a bit of a fall yesterday – nothing broken, luckily, which is something of a miracle, considering the old dear is not much more than a bag of bones - and she can't get out to do her shopping today. So I've put up a grocery order for her, and sent Ruth to pop it up to her cottage. I don't expect she'll be long."

"I'm sure we'll see her later," said Ron. "But in the meantime, what can you recommend for us in the way of pasties?"

A few minutes later, the purchase completed amongst a flurry of good wishes for a successful final performance, Tania and Ron emerged on to Fore Street. "Well, there goes Part A of your cunning plan," remarked Tania. "Ruth will have to go on the back burner."

"Don't speak too soon," riposted Ron. "Look who's just coming out of the pub." He nodded towards the front of the Pilchard's Arms, where Ruth Tresillian could be seen emerging and descending the steps, her face a picture of disappointment.

"Hello, Ruth," Tania greeted the young woman. "We've just been talking about you."

"Why? What about?" Ruth sounded alarmed.

"Oh, nothing to be worried about," Tania reassured her. "We've just been chatting to your uncle in his shop. We nipped in to buy some pasties to take home with us." Ron held up the bag containing the pasties as proof. "And he told us that you'd popped out to take some groceries to an old lady in the village."

"That's right," breathed Ruth. "Mrs Penrose couldn't get to the shop, so Uncle Abel sent me to deliver them to her." A tentative smile.

"And thence to the pub, apparently," smiled Ron. "Don't tell me that you've been escorting Mrs Penrose there in search of medicinal alcohol?" He grinned.

Ruth's face lost its smile. "No, nothing like that. I just ... I just wondered if Matthew might be there. I know they've been putting him up. Only I haven't seen him or Bianca since ..." She tailed off.

"You're fond of him, aren't you?" asked Tania delicately.

Ruth blushed. "Yes. And Bianca's a lovely little dog," she added hastily.

"If a little noisy at times," remarked Ron.

"Oh no, she never barks at me," said Ruth. "But that's probably because I'm always taking her little treats. Although Matt says she shouldn't really have bones because she's too small, but I tell him it's only natural for dogs to gnaw on bones, so I get little lamb chop bones from my uncle. And he doesn't mind really. That's why I was ..." Ruth broke off abruptly.

"Mmm?" murmured Tania quizzically.

"I mean, that's why I was asking at the Pilchard's," hurried on Ruth. "But Mary said Matt was out."

"We ran into him yesterday when we were out for a walk," said Tania. "He seemed alright, if a little down. It was the first time we'd had a chance to chat with him since Wednesday night, and I don't think I spoke with him then, because Simeon and he didn't stay very long at the party after the play. What a change from Tuesday night! I had a lovely long talk with him at the Feast before the Mumming. But of course, on Wednesday, things were a little different, what with ... well, you were there at the

White House before the performance, so you know."

"Yes." Ruth didn't seem disposed to be particularly forthcoming.

"And we hardly saw anything of you at the after-show party," pressed on Tania. "I think you must have left quite early yourself, didn't you? I expect you were tired." Ruth nodded wordlessly. "I wonder, did you go straight home?"

"Why do you ask?"

"Oh, no special reason," replied Tania airily. "It's just that I wondered if you might have seen anyone unexpectedly wandering about the village at that time of night. Luke, for instance. Because he was telling us that he'd had a sudden thought, and he'd gone back to the White House quite late on to make sure everything was properly locked up. We asked him the same question."

"And did he? See anyone?"

"No, nobody at all."

"Oh." Ruth's reaction was hard to gauge.

"Puzzling, isn't it? Because there must have been somebody about," pointed out Ron. "Somebody or something must have brought Simeon out of his house. And presumably had some sort of confrontation with him. But you didn't see anyone else on your way home?"

"No." Ruth shook her head. "Definitely not."

"Oh well." Ron shrugged. "We shall just have to keep on wondering, shan't we?"

*

"That didn't really tell us much," said Ron. "Apart from confirming the fact that the streets of Polkernow were not peopled by marauding gangs of sinister strangers on Wednesday night."

"No," mused Tania. "Ruth isn't exactly disposed to gossip, is she?"

"Whereas we know that Mary Pengelly seems ever-ready for a little light chat," smiled Ron. "And Ruth has just very helpfully informed us that she is to be found in the pub. So why don't we continue with Plan A, only slightly modified, and nip into the Pilchard's for a spot of lunch? Who knows, we may strike up a conversation."

"I'm not sure they'll take too kindly to us bringing our own pasties to the party," remarked Tania, indicating the bag Ron held.

"Bad etiquette, eh?" Ron laughed. "Take your point. Tell you what – give me two minutes to scoot up to the cottage and bung these in the fridge, and I'll be back to see if Mary has any light to shed on the case."

True to his word, Ron returned at a gentle jog a few minutes later, only slightly breathless, and the couple made their way into the bar of the Pilchard's Arms, where Mary Pengelly greeted them with her usual welcoming smile.

"Always for you, my loves," was her ready response to their enquiry as to whether lunch was still available. "Good job you weren't here earlier, because we were packed, but they all seemed to up and go at once, so we're blessedly quiet for the moment. So, would you like a look at the menu?"

Tania and Ron looked at one another. "Actually, I don't think we've gone far wrong with your recommendations so far," said Ron. "So what can you suggest for our last day? Preferably something typically Cornish."

"Oh well then, there's no contest," beamed Mary. "Angela's made a couple of lovely stargazy pies. Just the thing, and you couldn't get more Cornish than that."

"What on earth is a stargazy pie?" wondered Ron.

"You just take a seat in a booth, and I'll bring you out one to see." Mary vanished through the door to the kitchen, returning only moments later bearing a circular pie dish. The puff pastry crust, baked to an appetising golden brown, was pierced by a circle of eight pilchard heads poking up through it, and the whole creation gave off a delicious savoury aroma. "There you are, my loves," declared Mary triumphantly. "As Cornish as you please. Freshly caught pilchards, filleted and cooked in a lovely mustard and herb gravy. Now some folks are trying to get them called Cornish sardines, because they don't think the name 'pilchard' is modern enough, but we don't take any notice of that. Round here, they'll always be pilchards. Specially in this pub. And don't worry – you don't actually have to eat the heads. They're just decoration really."

"That's something of a relief," commented Tania. "I'm not that fond of food that looks at me while I'm eating it."

"I'm up for it," said Ron. "And if you can bake four-and-twenty blackbirds in a pie, why not a shoal of pilchards? So, two portions of stargazy pie, please."

*

"Unconventional but absolutely delicious," was Tania's verdict some while later, as she laid her cutlery down on a impressively clear plate. "And who knew kale went with fish?"

Ron looked up at the barmaid, who was just approaching to clear the table. "Mary, once again, my compliments. Your recommendations are flawless."

"And I bet you could manage a bowl of Cornish ice cream to finish off."

"You win the bet," laughed Ron.

Within minutes, the ice cream had arrived and been despatched, and Mary was once again appearing at the table. "Will you be wanting anything else?" she enquired.

Ron leaned back. "I couldn't manage another thing."

"Nor me," confirmed Tania. "Except ... perhaps a little chat."

196

"Oh? What about, my love?"

"Wednesday night."

Mary's eyes lit up. "Well, if you want to talk about that ..." She lowered her voice to such an extent that she virtually mouthed, "... there's a few things I could tell you as maybe you don't know. Trouble is, I'm working at the moment ..."

"Don't you believe a word of it," interrupted Toby Hayle, who had overheard Mary's words from behind the bar. "No point trying to be secret, Mary love. Ears like a bat, me." He laughed. "And the rush is over. I'm sure I can manage on my own, so why don't you take your break? Then you can sit down and have a little talk with our friends." He winked meaningfully in Tania's direction.

Mary didn't need to be told twice, and within moments she was sliding into the booth alongside Ron. "So, Wednesday night?"

"Well," began Tania, "we've been trying to work out who was where after the end of our party here ..."

"So's you could see who could have done for Simeon," said Mary. "That's how they do it on the telly, isn't it? Now me ..." She cleared her throat importantly. "I can account for my movements ..."

"Oh, we know where you went," stated Ron. "Your sister's already told us about the chocolate cake business."

"Poor love. She gets these awful heads," explained Mary. "Really knock her about, they do. She's had them ever since she was a teenager. The doctors do say it's a sign of high intelligence." She laughed. "That's probably why I never get them. But she was in a proper state, so I was only too pleased to step in and see to the cakes for her. And I'd only just finished clearing everything up and putting things away after setting the cakes to cool, when I heard the police siren going. 'What on earth's up?', I thought to myself. Course, I didn't know what it was at

197

the time. Well, we do now, don't we?"

"We do," nodded Tania. "I dare say Judith's husband will have told you all about it."

"Oh no," said Mary piously. "No, he's under orders not to discuss the case." She looked around to ensure that she couldn't be heard. "Mind you, that's not going to stop him telling his wife all about it, is it?" She dropped her voice to a whisper. "And she's not going to keep it from her sister, is she?"

"I imagine not," said Ron, stifling a smile. "So, what did she have to say?"

"Well, you'll be amazed," said Mary. She leaned forward confidentially. "The stuff these forensic people can tell you. Now, from what I heard, and I think it's pretty common knowledge, you found Simeon down on the theatre stage, dead, and stabbed with that quill of mine. So I bet you thought he'd been killed there."

"Well, obviously," replied Ron.

"No!" exclaimed Mary. "That's where you'd be wrong. Because the way Ben tells it, when they did the post-mortem, they found that Simeon had loads of broken bones and bruising, so the path-whatsisname ..."

"Forensic pathologist?" suggested Tania.

"That's right. So she came to the conclusion that Simeon had come by these injuries from falling all the way down to the stage from the top terrace."

"Oh, gosh." Tania was surprised. "Of course, we couldn't have known anything like that, on account of it being so dark when we found the body. So they think Simeon was stabbed up on the terrace, and then fell all the way down?"

"No! Wrong again! Because the forensic thingummy-woman said that there wasn't enough blood, and anyway, the quill would have been damaged if it had fallen all that way, and it wasn't. So she reckons that the quill was used to stab Simeon after he was dead."

There was a silence. "How bizarre," said Ron eventually. "Why on earth would someone do that?"

Mary shrugged. "I don't think they've worked that out yet." She suddenly chuckled. "And Ben said, they got into a fine old tizz about some bloodstain they found on the stage. Couldn't work it out, as it wasn't at the spot where the body was. So then they had it analysed. Turns out it wasn't Simeon's at all." The chuckle became a delighted laugh. "It was cow's blood!"

"But why on earth ...?" Tania thought for a moment, and then joined in the laughter. "Of course. Don't you remember, Ron? Ruth brought down some bones for Hamlet at rehearsal, and the bag was leaking."

"And that's how come the forensic people found a bag of little bones tucked away under the front row seats," continued Mary, "which was one of the things they couldn't figure out. And as for the ass's head, everybody's completely flummoxed."

Tania sat back, frowning. "I have to say, I'm feeling a bit that way myself. There's an awful lot there that doesn't seem to make sense."

"And it's not your job to do it," Ron gently reminded her. "Anyway, thank you for all that, Mary. But now, I think we ought to be getting on our way. We've got things to do back at the cottage, and we don't want to be in a last-minute rush for tonight's performance."

Chapter 19
Saturday

As Ron and Tania strolled hand-in-hand down through the village on their way to the Mandyke Theatre for the final performance, Ron couldn't help feeling that his wife was somewhat distracted. "What's up, love?" he enquired. "Feeling sad, now that the whole thing's almost over?"

Tania came back to herself with a start. "Sorry," she smiled. "I wasn't meaning to ignore you. It's just that I was thinking ..."

"About what?"

"And you're right, of course. In a way, I am going to be sorry that the play's finished. I mean, all that line-learning, and all those rehearsals, and now, after just a few evenings, our performances and our characters become part of the past instead of the future. But the audiences have been fantastic, and I'm sure everyone in the cast has had a wonderful time working together, so we really couldn't have hoped for better."

"I know what you mean," nodded Ron. "I've had people asking me in the past if I was sorry that whatever show I've been in was finished. And I've always said, if it's gone well, that it was a success, I had a good time, and now it's time to move on."

"Except ..."

"Except what?"

"It's fine for us Ramston people in the cast," said Tania, seeming to be searching for words. "We'll be gone tomorrow, and we may never come back to Polkernow again. We may even forget everything that's gone on this week. But for the people of Polkernow, it isn't over, is it? Unless and until somebody discovers what happened with Simeon, they're always going to be looking at one another and wondering."

"And we know, and they know, that every one of them connected with our play had some reason to dislike Simeon. But it's a far cry from that to actually wanting him dead."

"I know, I know." Tania gave a rueful laugh. "Maddening, isn't it?"

"So here's what I suggest," said her husband firmly. "Let's try and shake this off, for tonight at least. Let's think about all the good stuff, like David and Elizabeth's boys almost going off pop with pride on the first night, or James virtually stopping the show with his antics as Lion, or the fight scene between Esther and Sarah that had the audience cheering them on. And I swear I caught Leah wiping away a tear of pride when we were taking the opening night curtain call. So let's just concentrate on giving tonight's crowd a performance they'll always remember."

"You're right." Tania leaned in to Ron and kissed him. She looked around at the groups and couples dotted around the streets, and the steady stream of people coming down from the car park, all doubtless heading for the theatre. "Let's go and give them hell."

In a considerable feat of synchronicity, as Ron and Tania came past the Pilchard's Arms, they were joined by the four youngsters and Andrew emerging from the pub, while Peter and Martha Talbot could be seen approaching from the other direction, with Susannah being towed as usual by an eager Hamlet, with the Kent family and their children, accompanied by Thomas and James, not far behind. As the group congregated at the top of the lane to the White House, Leah emerged from the entrance to her flat above the cafe, and the company was complete.

"I'm glad you're all here," said Leah, after greetings had been exchanged. "I want a word with everyone before Reuben calls the half this evening. So let's head on down, away from the throng, and we can gather on the stage for a brief chat." And she led the way towards the theatre with a purposeful stride, while the rest of the company followed on behind in an untidy straggle, exchanging tales of what they had been doing over the past hours and days.

"Right, you lot," said Leah, standing on one of the low platforms on stage, as the others gathered around her. "Slight change of plan from the usual. There will be no get-out work-party after tonight's performance."

There was a slight groan from the company. "Does that mean we're going to have to come in and do it in the morning?" enquired Andrew. "Surely that's going to put a lot of people's plans out."

"Nothing of the sort," smiled Leah in reassurance. "Because I've been having a word with Reuben, and he tells me that the company coming in for next week's show won't be arriving until Monday. So he has volunteered to rustle up some helpers to put everything on my van first thing tomorrow, leaving all of you free tonight ... for a party! Courtesy of the Mandyke Theatre management." Frowns were instantly replaced by grins of delight, and there was even a small cheer. "So, with that in mind, go and enjoy yourselves tonight."

"And this," announced Reuben, appearing as if by magic at Leah's shoulder, "ladies and gentlemen, is your half-hour call."

The warning bell sounded from the White House above, and the cast dispersed chattering to their dressing-rooms.

*

Ron's brisk 'Come in!' in response to the tap at the dressing-room door was followed by Naomi Constantine's appearance in the doorway. "Reuben sent me round to give everyone their 'Beginners please' call," she announced. "And he says to tell everyone 'Break a leg'."

"Thanks, Naomi," said Ron. "How come you're doing the call tonight? It's usually the A.S.M.'s job."

"Oh, Ruth was checking something in the props room," said Naomi. "Apparently one of the props had gone astray."

"Lord! Hope it's not my magic flower," remarked Ron. "That'll throw the whole plot into confusion. Nobody'll know who's supposed to be in love with whom!"

"I think it's all sorted now," smiled Naomi. "Whatever it was. Anyway, I'd better get back to my perch."

"How's the house?" enquired Tania. "Although I don't suppose I need to ask, after we've been told there's not a seat to be had."

"Nicely packed," replied Naomi. "I had a peep just now." She made to leave, but then stopped. "Oh, I'll tell you one thing I noticed. In the two house seats right at the back. Those two policemen. Inspector Tregarth and Sergeant Mitchell are sitting up there looking rather stern."

"Maybe Shakespeare isn't their scene," quipped Ron. "Or else they're revisiting the scene of the crime, in the hope that the murderer will reveal themselves in some dramatic fashion during the performance."

"Oh, do shut up, Ron," said Tania with a touch of asperity. "Simeon's death is the last thing we need to be reminded of at the moment. We've got a play to do."

"Sorry, darling," apologised Ron. "Anyway, don't let us keep you, Naomi. You've got things to do. As have we." He got to his feet and held out a hand to his wife. "Come, my dearest Queen of the Amazons. Let's go and dazzle the Athenian court."

Despite her words, Tania couldn't help odd disconnected thoughts arising in her mind as the play

203

progressed. From the opening scene, when Paul delivered Lysander's line *'The course of true love never did run smooth'*, to the moment in the scene in the forest when Ron, in his character as Duke of Athens, firmly holding on to Hamlet's leash as the dog strained forwards, praised Theseus' hunting hounds and their bell-like cry, random reflections circulated in one part of her mind as she tried to give her main concentration to her performance. What exactly was the nature of the relationship between Simeon and Matthew? With so many people having run foul of Simeon, and with him holding so many unfavourable opinions of the theatre's support team, how on earth had he managed to retain his position as artistic director? Did he have some sort of hold over someone which only his death could loose? And what on earth put thoughts of the butcher's description of old Mrs Penrose into her head? How could that possibly relate to the forensic team's findings? And what was the reason for the bizarre theatricality of the death scene? What was the relevance of the ass's head and the bronze quill? She was struck by the lines delivered by Martha as Quince, presenting the prologue of the comic play within-the-play, when she spoke of Pyramus as *'with bloody baleful blade, He bravely broached his boiling bloody breast!'*. Except, of course, for the conflicting evidence of the blood, or its lack. Overall, Susannah's words as Puck, as he mocked the tangled and confused lovers, kept coming back to her – *'Lord, what fools these mortals be!'*. And in the final scene of the play, as she delivered her own line *'I love not to see wretchedness o'er-charged'*, she experienced a sudden flash of illumination that brought all the elements of the situation home to her.

She could hardly wait for the dressing-room door to close behind her and Ron after a lengthy and enthusiastic curtain-call before turning to her husband with shining eyes and exclaiming excitedly, "I think I know what happened!"

"We all just gave a damn good performance, that's what happened," grinned Ron with a mixture of triumph and relief, as he started to change out of his costume.

"No, you idiot! I mean with Simeon. I think I know how he died, and why."

Ron regarded her with astonishment. "You do? Well, come on – spill the beans."

Tania hesitated. "Not just yet. I have to piece it all together, and there's still quite a lot of guesswork. But I'm sure I'm right."

"So hadn't you better tell Inspector Tregarth?"

Tania sighed. "But it's going to put a damper on the whole evening. And I don't want to spoil everything for all the others, especially Leah."

Ron thought for a moment. "How about this? There's this get-together up at the White House. Why don't you somehow slip a word to the inspector that you've got something to tell him and suggest that he hangs around, and then, at the end of the party, when everybody has had their celebration, tell him what you have to say?"

Tania nodded. "That sounds good."

"And you're sure you can't give me just a hint?" wheedled Ron.

"Not until I've had a chance to think everything through properly," insisted Tania. "Although ..." She relented slightly. "You could give some thought to that play we went to see in London."

"Which one?"

"'*The Curious Incident Of The Dog In The Night-time*'."

"Oh, that's a great help!" responded Ron with a perplexed laugh. "Very well then, woman of mystery," he continued, smiling. "In that case, get yourself ready for the party. I have a suspicion that you've probably bagged yourself another leading rôle."

"Never mind about that," said Tania. "I'm not sure why Inspector Tregarth is here, but shouldn't somebody make sure that he doesn't leave?"

"Good point. Give me two seconds." Ron virtually threw his clothes on and sprinted out of the dressing-room, leaving Tania deep in thought.

*

"Well, that's that," declared Luke Crowan, as he came in through the front door of the White House and locked it behind him. "The play is officially over. The audience have all gone, and Ben Polkerris here has seen the last of the cars out of the lane, with no ructions between drivers at all, much to his surprise." The constable alongside him, slightly stiff in his uniform, gave a self-conscious grin. "So please, as we're all off duty now, dig in!"

Those present didn't need a second invitation and, once the entire cast and crew gathered together in the cafe had begun to make inroads into the spread of snacks and drinks laid out by Judith Polkerris and Mary Pengelly, Reuben Hawke tapped his glass for silence. "Now that, as stage manager for 'A Midsummer Night's Dream', I'm almost out of a job ..." There was a quiet ripple of amusement. "... I'd like to thank Leah and all her company for doing the theatre, and the village, proud with your production. We've thoroughly enjoyed having you as our guests. And it's also a pleasure to welcome a few extra guests for our little get-together this evening before you all disperse – Angela Hayle's managed to escape from her pub kitchen, I can see Naomi's parents over there, and also Ruth's uncle and aunt." He turned to Luke. "What a shame your own Aunt Demelza couldn't make it, Luke. I expect something unforeseen cropped up." A chuckle from the locals. "I'm also pleased that Matt has felt able to be here." All eyes turned towards Matthew Sutcombe, standing slightly apart, Angela's arm around him protectively. "And we mustn't forget the two gentlemen we weren't expecting to join us in Polkernow this week, and who have become an unanticipated part of our lives." A dry smile. "Sergeant Mitchell and Inspector Tregarth. Who, I believe, has something to say." He stepped aside.

"I simply wanted," announced Inspector Tregarth, "to express my thanks to everyone for the co-operation you've given to myself and my colleagues during what I realise has been a difficult time for all of you. And I was slightly surprised to have been asked to join your gathering this evening ..." He flicked a sideways glance in Tania's direction. "... but at least it gives me a chance to congratulate you all on a fine performance. And to assure you, Miss Sutherland, and the rest of your acting company, that none of you are regarded as being in any way involved in this week's tragedy. That is the pleasant part." His face grew solemn. "But I'm afraid, despite what Mr. Crowan said just now, not all of us are off duty. And in amongst all the positives, I'm afraid that the death of Mr. Ashton-Rose has cast a pall." The atmosphere in the room grew perceptibly chillier. "Now tonight, very much to my surprise, I had a very informative conversation with a member of the company. They hinted that they had some insights into the situation, which they would explain to me later. However, I wasn't prepared to wait, and I insisted. They made a very compelling case. In my opinion, everyone here has an interest in bringing this sad matter to a conclusion. And so, unconventional though it may be, I'm going to ask them to explain to you what they have told me." He stepped back. "So over to you ... Mrs Faye."

"Me?" Tania was startled. "But ... but I can't ... I mean, it wouldn't be right ..." She faltered to a halt.

"You know the ins and outs of this play far better than I ever will," insisted Tregarth. "And it's the play that's brought you to what I accept must be the truth. So please ... explain."

Tania took a deep breath, cast a look at Ron who gave her a nod of reassurance, and began. "The whole situation is all about love – love gone right and love gone wrong. And from what we were told, plenty of the local people had no great reason to love Simeon Ashton-Rose. But whether all their various problems with him were sufficient for them to wish him dead, that's another matter. The thing is, when you love somebody, and you see them threatened in some way, that could provoke a very powerful instinct, a wish to protect them. So Judith was accused of financial irregularity, while her husband's job could have been at risk if Simeon's pursuit of him had succeeded. Either of them might have wished Simeon out of the way. Reuben was another whose financial honesty was questioned by Simeon. Who amongst you might stand up for him? Again, Judith's sister was on the receiving end of Simeon's attacks – might Mary have come to her sister's defence? Or, again, could Judith have felt the need to protect Mary from Simeon's determination to remove her from her much-loved position with the theatre company?"

"Are you seriously suggesting that my sister and I might have cooked up some plot to kill Simeon because of the nasty stories he'd been spreading about us?" queried Judith hotly.

"I'm only considering what the police might have thought, if these things had come to their ears," responded Tania. "Although I have a feeling that most of them never did." In the background, Inspector Tregarth nodded in agreement, his eyebrows raised in surprise at some of Tania's revelations. "And there were other possibilities," she continued. "Take Naomi and Luke.

Naomi had been accused of incompetence, while Luke had stood in danger of investigation because of some unwarranted smears on Simeon's part. Either might act to defend the other. And one major problem is that none of these people could prove that they were nowhere near the White House at the relevant time. Indeed, Luke has admitted that he was. But in the case of Matthew, of course, it's a very different matter."

"You surely don't think Matt had anything to do with this?" demanded Angela Hayle, her arm tightening around the young man's shoulder.

Tania smiled faintly. "I don't. Largely because, in all of this, Matthew is the only person who has had anything at all good to say about Simeon. Not that he was necessarily rewarded for his loyalty. We've all witnessed the way Simeon was capable of treating him. But then my thoughts returned to our play, and the theme of love. Matthew, I believe, did love Simeon, despite the other man's asinine treatment of him. But there was someone who loved Matthew more than Simeon probably ever did. And I was reminded of that right at the start of tonight's performance when Paul, speaking of the character of Helena, delivered Lysander's line *'And she, sweet lady, dotes, devoutly dotes, dotes in idolatry, upon this man'*. That couldn't be more true of anyone than Ruth Tresillian. Or, as somebody described her to me, 'poor Ruth'."

Chapter 20
Saturday

"Ruth?" There was a gasp all around the room.

"You surely can't mean that." Reuben voiced the general incredulity.

Tania shook her head sadly. "I'm afraid so. I couldn't bring myself to think otherwise."

"But why?" Naomi sounded stunned.

As Ruth's uncle and aunt closed in protectively around their niece, Tania cast a look of appeal in the direction of Inspector Tregarth. "Inspector, I don't think I can do this."

"You're doing very well, Mrs Faye," replied the inspector. "Far better, I suspect, than I could have done. And I have a feeling that your friends will accept your deductions much more easily than they would have from me. So please, carry on."

Tania took another slightly shaky breath and gathered her thoughts. "It wasn't just the content of the play, although that was the main element of my thinking. But then there were other questions that kept nagging at me. Why hadn't Bianca reacted, when there was obviously some kind of intruder in the moments leading up to Simeon's death? I couldn't help remembering the Sherlock Holmes story, where the most significant fact was that the dog *didn't* bark in the night. We'd been told so often, and heard for ourselves, how readily she barks when anybody is around. But then Ruth told me herself how, unlike the dog's reaction to everyone else, Bianca never barks at her. Because she's so used to her. She regards her as a special friend. Perhaps that's because, as Ruth also mentioned to me, she is always taking her little treats. Like, for instance, the bag of small bones which the police forensic people found at the scene. Not the large beef bones which Ruth had previously provided for

Hamlet, which leaked that misleading bloodstain on the stage, and which had already been taken backstage, but small lamb bones for a small dog. I wondered how those bones had got there. And I realised that the only person who could have brought them to the scene was Ruth, with her access to the stock of the butcher's shop. But why would she be present at the theatre so late that night? I felt that it must hark back to the incident at the beginning of the evening, when Simeon had delivered that humiliating slap to Matthew in front of everybody. She would have seen that Matthew was still upset at the after-show party, so she must have tried to think of a way to cheer him up. And the thought must have formed in her mind, that one way to do so was to bring some little treats for Bianca, the pet he loves so much."

All eyes came to rest on Ruth, who had listened to Tania's relation in a state of stunned stillness. Suddenly her composure broke, and she began to sob. "I never meant ..." She caught her breath, and continued in a firmer voice. "I never meant for Simeon to die."

An even more profound silence settled over the room, broken by Inspector Tregarth, who stepped up to Ruth's side. "Perhaps you'd better tell us what happened," he suggested, in a surprisingly gentle voice.

Ruth took a handkerchief from her sleeve, wiped her eyes, and looked around the room. "I'm so sorry, everyone, for the trouble I've caused you all. Especially you, Matthew. And Tania is right in everything she says. I did come here after the show party on Wednesday night. And really, I did only mean to leave that little parcel of bones for Matthew to find on Thursday morning. He'd have known they came from me. But it was just bad luck – just as I reached the back terrace, Simeon came out on to his balcony and caught me. And he said 'What the hell are you doing here, girl?' And I said 'Nothing. I was just ...', but he interrupted and said 'You stay right there. I'm

211

coming down, and we'll sort this out once and for all'. And a few moments later, he came out on to the terrace."

Tregarth looked at Matthew. "And you weren't aware of this?"

Matthew shook his head. "I must have been asleep. And if it was Simeon moving about in the house, I don't think Bianca would have reacted."

"Go on, Miss Tresillian," said the inspector.

"He came out on to the terrace," continued Ruth with a sigh, "and he was in a terrible rage. He grabbed me. Asked what on earth I was playing at. Suggested that I was sneaking around in some pathetic attempt to catch a glimpse of Matthew. He asked me what I was carrying, so I told him, and he said that if I thought I had the remotest chance of wheedling my way into Matt's affections with little presents for his lapdog, I must be insane. He said that this week's play was the perfect illustration of my stupidity. I tried to explain. I said I couldn't help myself. I tried to tell him about the heartache I felt, but he just sneered. He called me a fool. He said I was exactly like Titania, ridiculously in love with someone absurdly wrong for her, except that I was the ass. And he told me to get out and never come back – that I'd never be allowed to set foot in his theatre ever again." The tears began to flow once more.

"And what happened next?" prompted Tresillian.

"He tried to push me out," said Ruth. "But he said that I might as well do one last useful thing before I went, and leave the bones for Bianca, if only to keep her quiet for five minutes. He grabbed them from me, and I tried to get them back, and we were struggling together, and all of a sudden we were at the top of the steps, and his foot went backwards into nothing, and he reached out to me, and I just instinctively snatched my hand away, and ... he fell. All the way down the steps, right down on to the stage. And he just lay there, not moving." Ruth's eyes widened as she relived the moment.

A hush fell, which seemed as if it would last forever until it was broken by Tania's voice. "Go on, Ruth," she coaxed gently.

"I went down to see him, but he didn't move at all. And it was so dark, I couldn't tell if he was alive or what, and then ..." Ruth looked around the room and shrugged helplessly. "I don't know why I did what I did. I suppose it was some kind of madness. I just remembered all the things Simeon had said to me, and I must have wanted to transform him into the fool that he'd called me. I ran to the wings, got my headband torch that I keep there, and went to the props room to fetch the ass's head. And next to it was lying the quill, and I picked that up too. Then I went back and put the head on to Simeon. Now who was the ridiculous one? And then ... oh, it's horrible to think of it ... I truly must have gone mad ... I remembered that he'd dismissed my talk of heartache, and I thought 'And that makes you heartless, so this won't hurt a bit'." Ruth's face crumpled in misery. "And then I stabbed him with the quill, straight to the heart. And then I ran home and hid in my room and tried to pretend that none of it had ever happened." She looked towards Matthew. "And I'm so so sorry."

Everyone present stood as if frozen, stunned into immobility by Ruth's revelations, until Inspector Tregarth cleared his throat. "Miss Tresillian, I think you'd better come with us." He turned to his detective colleague. "Sergeant Mitchell, perhaps you would attend to the formalities."

Mitchell stepped forward and took Ruth gently by the arm. "Ruth Tresillian," he began, "I am arresting you ..."

His superior interrupted him. "Outside, I think, sergeant. There's no need to make things even worse by embarrassing the entire gathering."

"Very good, sir." The sergeant indicated to Ruth to move towards the front door, as Luke Crowan hurried to unlock it ahead of him, and Ruth's uncle and aunt, huddled together in shock, fell in behind them.

The inspector approached Tania. "Thank you, Mrs Faye. And well done. I know that can't have been easy."

"I don't know that congratulations are in order, Mr Tregarth," replied Tania shakily. "And no, it wasn't easy at all. And I'm still not sure I understand why you wanted me to do it."

"Because," said Tregarth, "I think, coming from me, the whole matter would have been so much more formal. More threatening. Harder for everyone to hear. But when you explained things, it became somehow gentler."

"I wouldn't have thought you'd allow yourself to worry about such things," said Tania, surprised.

"Maybe," responded the inspector, with the unexpected hint of a twinkle, "I'm not such an ogre as I like to pretend." He stepped back and shook Tania's hand. "Anyway, thank you once again. And now, if you'll excuse me, I have duties to attend to." With a brief wordless nod to those present, he strode from the room.

*

The next morning, having just finished putting the last of their things in the car, and being about to start one final circuit of Hollyhock Cottage to ensure that nothing had been left behind, Ron was surprised by the knock at the front door. He opened it, to find Leah Sutherland standing on the doorstep.

"Goodness, Leah, you cut that fine," said Tania, as Ron ushered their visitor into the sitting room. "Another couple of minutes and we'd have been gone."

"Me too," said Leah. "I was just about to take my van down to the theatre for Reuben and his team to load up our stuff, but I wanted to have a quick word with you first."

"Have you heard what's happening?" enquired Ron.

"That's one thing about being in a small village," smiled Leah drily. "The news goes round at the speed of light. So Mary Pengelly has told me, having got it from her sister, who got it from her husband Ben, that they're not certain exactly what Ruth is going to be charged with. Because if Simeon was already dead when she stabbed him, and if his fall was accidental, then they're on shaky ground with a charge of murder. I hope they don't put the poor girl though the mill too much. She's been through enough."

Tania nodded. "You may be right."

"But I'm still not absolutely sure," continued Leah, "how it was that you suddenly realised, during the course of last night's show, what had actually happened."

Tania thought for a moment. "I suppose, in a way, you could say it was all thanks to Hamlet."

"Hamlet?" Leah sounded amazed. "What on earth has Hamlet got to do with it? Either the Prince or the dog?"

"It was those bones that the police team found under the front row of seats," explained Tania. "I knew they couldn't be for Peter's Great Dane, because his had already been removed from the stage. But Ruth had mentioned her treats for Bianca, and we now know, from what she said last night, that Simeon had snatched her parcel from her just before he fell. It must have flown from his hand when he landed on the stage, and that's how it ended up where it did. The final piece of the jigsaw."

Leah shook her head in gentle disbelief. "Well, my girl, I don't think anyone could have worked it out the way you did. You must have a talent for these things. And now I must be getting on, or else Reuben will be getting twitchy. So I'll see you two back at the next meeting of the Society in Ramston. We'll have to be making a start

215

choosing our next production." She made her way out of the front door and into Fore Street, but paused as she closed the gate behind her. "I've just had a wonderful idea. There's a very funny musical whodunnit called 'Something's Afoot', with a marvellous leading rôle as a female amateur detective. Tania, you'd be perfect for it!"

"Oh no," laughed Tania. "After this week, I'm sticking to pot-boiler comedies. I think a good light-hearted production of 'Whoops, There Go My Trousers' is much more my cup of tea."

"We'll see," said Leah, nodding sagely. "We'll see."

* * *

also by Roger Keevil

The Inspector Constable Murder Mysteries

Murderer's Fête
Who could have foreseen the murder of a clairvoyant at a country fête?

Murder Unearthed
Sun, sangria and suspects during a supposed holiday in Spain

Death Sails In The Sunset
Murder ensues when a journalist won't let guilty secrets be buried at sea

Murder Comes To Call
Three short stories to tax the talents of our detectives

Murder Most Frequent
Another trilogy of intriguing cases for Constable and Copper

The Odds On Murder
Who is riding for a fall when a prominent racehorse trainer is killed?

No Bar To Murder
Complicated relationships make a potent and lethal cocktail

The Murder Cabinet
A return to Dammett Hall leaves the nation's fate in the team's hands

The Game Of Murder
Sudden death at the TV studio as entertainment turns to murder;
PLUS a bonus short story, 'Exit A Murderer',
and a full index to all the Inspector Constable mysteries

The Copper & Co Murder Mysteries

Honeymooner's Murder
Even on an idyllic tropical island, murder never takes a holiday

Murder At Witch's Holt
Dark secrets lead to a strange death at a spooky manor house

Buccaneer's Murder
A wealthy businessman lies dead aboard his luxury private yacht

* * *

Printed in Great Britain
by Amazon

58399010R00126